The Last G.I. Bride Wore Tartan

Also by Fred Urquhart

Novels
TIME WILL KNIT
THE FERRET WAS ABRAHAM'S DAUGHTER*
JEZEBEL'S DUST*
PALACE OF GREEN DAYS

Short Stories
I FELL FOR A SAILOR*
THE CLOUDS ARE BIG WITH MERCY*
SELECTED STORIES
THE YEAR OF THE SHORT CORN*
THE LAST SISTER
THE LAUNDRY GIRL AND THE POLE
THE DYING STALLION
THE PLOUGHING MATCH
PROUD LADY IN A CAGE
A DIVER IN CHINA SEAS*
SEVEN GHOSTS IN SEARCH*
FULL SCORE (edited by Graeme Roberts)
A GOAL FOR MISS VALENTINO**

Edited Books
NO SCOTTISH TWILIGHT (with Maurice Lindsay)
W.S.C.: A CARTOON BIOGRAPHY
GREAT TRUE WAR ADVENTURES
MEN AT WAR
SCOTTISH SHORT STORIES
GREAT TRUE ESCAPE STORIES
THE CASSELL MISCELLANY, 1848-1958
MODERN SCOTTISH SHORT STORIES (with Giles Gordon)
THE BOOK OF HORSES

Other
SCOTLAND IN COLOUR (with Kenneth Scowen)
EVERYMAN'S DICTIONARY OF FICTIONAL CHARACTERS
(with William Freeman)

* Reprinted with new introductions in this series by Kennedy & Boyd
**First publication in THE FRED URQUHART COLLECTION

The Last G.I. Bride Wore Tartan

Fred Urquhart

WITH AN INTRODUCTION BY
COLIN AFFLECK

Kennedy & Boyd
an imprint of
Zeticula Ltd
Unit 13
196 Rose Street
Edinburgh, EH2 4AT
Scotland.

http://www.kennedyandboyd.co.uk
admin@kennedyandboyd.co.uk

First published in 1948 in Edinburgh by Serif Books
Reprinted with corrections 2022
Text Copyright © Estate of Fred Urquhart 2022
Introduction Copyright © Colin Affleck 2022

Front cover image Copyright © Zeticula 2022
Back cover photograph from Fred Urquhart's own collection
Copyright © Colin Affleck 2022

ISBN 978-1-84921-106-2

All rights reserved. No part of this publication may be reproduced, stored in a retrieval system, or transmitted in any form or by any means, electronic, mechanical, photocopying, recording or otherwise, without the prior permission of the publishers.

For

José Wilson

Acknowledgements

Some of these stories have appeared in *Tribune* and *Woman's Own*, and I wish to make the usual acknowledgements to the editors.

Contents

Introduction *by Colin Affleck*	ix
The Last G.I. Bride Wore Tartan	13
Hunt the Slipper	58
I Married Three Actresses	69
Call Me Blondie	80
But German Girls Walk Different	87
The Dream Book	95
The Jolly Garçon	105

Introduction

I found my first copy of *The Last G.I. Bride Wore Tartan* at a book sale, where it had been mistakenly placed in the American History section; but this was not entirely inappropriate, since it is the most obviously American-influenced of Fred Urquhart's collections of short stories. There are some American characters in this book, and many others speak in an Americanised idiom and make references to American culture. The informal style and snappy dialogue reflect American models, cinematic as much as literary. Urquhart had used these features in several earlier stories, and half of the chapters in his first novel, *Time Will Knit* (1938), are narrated by Spike, an American sailor. Urquhart named a number of U.S. writers who were early influences on his work, including Ernest Hemingway, William Saroyan and Erskine Caldwell; he also read 'countless' American magazines, such as *The Saturday Evening Post*; and from his early years he spent very many hours watching Hollywood films. In an autobiographical sketch he wrote, 'In my teens and early twenties, although I'd never been out of Scotland, I knew more about the American way of life than I did about the Scottish.'[1] This book does, however, include some of the realistic Scottish dialogue for which Urquhart was well known.

On 24 February 1947 Urquhart sent his novella 'The Last G.I. Bride Wore Tartan' to William Fordie Forrester, the Scottish representative of Methuen, the firm which was to publish four of Urquhart's books between 1949 and 1951. Forrester passed it on to Joseph Stanley Mardel, the owner of the new Edinburgh publisher Serif Books,[2] who was interested in publishing it, but some additional stories were needed to make a book. On 8 March Urquhart sent six that were already written but had not yet been allocated to a collection. The original intention was to bring the book out during the first Edinburgh International Festival in 1947 and the first edition shows that as the year of publication, but it was actually published on 26 January 1948.[3]

Urquhart's acknowledgements relating to the first publication of some of the stories are to two periodicals, *Tribune* and *Woman's Own*,[4] which one would not expect to see in conjunction: a left-wing Labourite journal and a popular women's magazine. Urquhart had been contributing stories, articles and reviews to the former for several years before he became in autumn 1946 its temporary literary editor (standing in for Tosco Fyvel, who had succeeded George Orwell). Since he had described himself as a communist and had been seen as a 'proletarian' writer, it is not surprising that Urquhart should form a connection with *Tribune*.

After the Second World War, Urquhart was trying to find new outlets for his stories. In June or July 1946 he sent a copy of his collection *The Clouds Are Big with Mercy*, along with the story 'Everybody Has Somebody Else',[5] which had appeared in the American magazine *Harper's Bazaar*, to James Wedgwood Drawbell, the distinguished Scottish journalist who had just become managing editor of *Woman's Own*, for which he had ambitious plans. Drawbell wanted to employ a better class of writer:

> I thought it would be fun in that grim world of 1946 to make a magazine that would be ... filled, not with the old-fashioned fiction suitable for the cabman's wife, but with the popular writers of our time – Somerset Maugham, H. E. Bates, Scott Fitzgerald, Pearl Buck, A. J. Cronin, Daphne du Maurier, John O'Hara, William Saroyan, Nigel Bulchin [*sic*], Vicki Baum, Carson McCullers, Elizabeth Taylor (not the film star!), Morley Callaghan, Mrs. Robert Henrey, Fred Urquhart and Noel Coward.[6]

Drawbell accepted 'Everybody Has Somebody Else', which, revised and re-named 'Nobody's Baby', appeared in the edition of 18 October 1946. This was the first of a number of stories that Urquhart contributed to the magazine. Some of these he considered to be 'rubbish' and did not include in his collections – such stories were written just for money (*Woman's Own* paid 25 guineas or so for a story, quite a large amount) – but others were of a higher literary quality. *Woman's Own* built up Urquhart's image, with photographs and snippets about him. In spring 1947 he attended the *Woman's Own* party at the Savoy, along with such celebrities as Jean Kent and Leslie Arliss, and got drunk with José Wilson, the magazine's fiction editor, with whom he had quickly become friends (and to whom this volume is dedicated).[7]

*

G.I. brides were in the news in 1946. From January of that year, special 'bride ships', provided by the U.S. Government free of charge, carried across the Atlantic British women who had married American servicemen. It is estimated that about 70,000 of these war brides went to the U.S.A. This migration continued up to the end of 1950, although 'the last official war bride ship, the *Henry Gibbons*, left Southampton' in October 1946.[8] It seems likely that the latter fact inspired Urquhart to write his highly amusing novella 'The Last G.I. Bride Wore Tartan'. It rushes along as the eighteen-year-old Jessie McIntyre tells how she left her Scottish village after the end of the Second World War and went 'to London to get a Yank,' before they all went home: 'I wasn't half mad, I can tell you, that the War hadn't lasted a bit longer.'

Through her story Urquhart expresses a satirical view of the saturation of British popular culture by American influences. The young people speak in an adapted American idiom that they have evidently learnt from the 'movies'; Jessie still uses some Scottish expressions ('I was fair away with myself'), while her mother, in contrast, speaks completely in vivid Scots. Jessie sees the characters played by Hollywood stars as models to be imitated, so she laughs like Hedy Lamarr, although she is too scared to talk like Carole Lombard when the opportunity arises in a radio interview and can't actually say anything. She continually re-reads Anita Loos's *Gentlemen Prefer Blondes*, which she has evidently mistaken for a self-improvement book rather than a satirical novel, and she tries to behave like its gold-digging heroine, Lorelei Lee. (Urquhart's story could be seen as a similarly breathless, Scottish version of Loos's book, a supposedly naïve first person narrative in which the heroine sails across the Atlantic and makes an advantageous marriage.)

Jessie says that her plan is to marry a G.I. and thus be transported to the U.S.A., where she will get a divorce and then find stardom in Hollywood.[9] After being given another book that provides a guide to American life – *A Bride's Guide to the U.S.A.*

(a genuine pamphlet for G.I. brides, published by *Good Housekeeping Magazine* and the United States Office of War Information)[10] – she sails for America. Urquhart conveys well the doubts and worries that assailed the women in this situation; Jessie realises that her husband 'was more or less a stranger'. Once she gets to Minnesota, Urquhart turns his satire on the Americans, such as a snobbish matron who loves the Royal Family and an old man of Scottish descent obsessed with the clichés of his ancestral homeland. It is also amusing to see these surroundings through Jessie's eyes; she remarks that her father-in-law's shop is 'almost as big as a Woolworth's in Perth or Dundee'. She keeps insisting that she is 'hard', but it becomes evident from her self-revealing narrative that the Americanised carapace she has adopted is not her real self, although she never ceases to use stars like Ginger Rogers and Bette Davis as points of reference.

Despite the satire, it is evident that Urquhart loves the exuberance of American culture and of Jessie, and the reader is always on her side. With her tartan skirt, the badge of Scottishness, she is wonderfully irrepressible, right to the very end of her story.

This piece is part of a succession of works in which Urquhart dealt with young Scottish women pursuing (and being pursued by) foreign soldiers. The earlier novella 'Namiętność – or The Laundry Girl and the

Pole'[11] shows the interaction between Polish soldiers stationed in a small Scottish town and the young women there; although the latter are influenced by the images of Hollywood film stars such as Greta Garbo and Joan Crawford, their language is much more Scottish than Jessie's and seems unaffected by the U.S.A. In Urquhart's later novels *The Ferret Was Abraham's Daughter* (1949) and *Jezebel's Dust* (1951), the young women chasing servicemen, including Poles and Americans, use more Americanisms, but their language is predominantly Scots. Although the second book also contains a G.I. bride, the draw of the U.S.A. is not the focus as it is in 'The Last G.I. Bride Wore Tartan'.

Urquhart sent Mardel a letter about alterations (by the printers) to the text in the proofs of the book, which is revealing about his methods and intentions. He quotes a passage from 'The Last G.I. Bride Wore Tartan' as he wrote it:

> 'Aw, what's the hurry,' he said.
> 'Do you remember that last night in London?' he said.
> 'Will I ever forget it,' I said.
> 'That's the way I feel now,' he said.
> 'That's the way I'll always feel about you, baby,' he said.

This layout, with continuous speech by the same person divided into separate paragraphs and repetition of 'he said / I said', occurs in many of Urquhart's early stories. One effect of it is to suggest pauses (and possibly actions) between the paragraphs. He complained to Mardel that the first and second paragraphs here had been joined and also the fourth and fifth, and this more conventional layout had been adopted throughout the book. In addition, it was being suggested that the repeated 'he said / I said' should be removed in each case. Urquhart said he was undoing these changes for stylistic reasons:

> I have asked a number of people, who had already read the story in typescript, what they thought about these alterations, and they are all agreed that I must stick to the way in which I originally wrote it, otherwise the book would lose its 'flavour.' After all, it is supposed to be either written or spoken by an illiterate girl, and that is the way illiterate people speak (and also write – when they can write). It seems to me that the short paragraphs with the reiterated 'he said' or 'I said' give the reader some idea of all the undercurrents that were going on. I propose, therefore, to alter everything back to the way I had it in my typescript. After all, I am not the only writer who does these short paragraphs of reiterated dialogue (there's always Hemingway as an example!).[12]

Urquhart evidently did not get his own way entirely, since the last two lines quoted have still been put into one paragraph in the published text (see page 57). It should be pointed out that Urquhart does not only use this technique when dealing with 'illiterate' characters; see, among many examples, the second and third complete paragraphs on page 109 of this book (in 'The Jolly Garçon').

Three other stories relate in varying degrees to Hollywood films. 'I Married Three Actresses' is a totally American story, in setting, characters and the hard-boiled language and style. Hank, a musician, tells the story of his career and his three marriages: to a singer, a sixteen stone 'Burlesque Queen', and an actress on the legitimate stage. His narrative reads like the voice-over in a film noir; Urquhart reproduces the atmosphere of those 1940s Hollywood crime films, with a cynical tone and references to sex, although the reason that Hank kills his third wife is not something that Hollywood of that period would have explicitly mentioned. There is some sly humour present; Hank's band is called Natasha and the Three Nimble-Wits, then it descends to Bertha and the Three Bumble-Wits.

In 'Call Me Blondie' a workman called Mac is attempting to decorate a room in the house of the ageing and predatory Mrs Ames, whose husband is 'travelling down Kilmarnock way'. She says that she goes to 'the pictures'; it would appear that she has been to see too many films like *Double Indemnity* or *The Postman Always Rings Twice*, since she tries to talk and behave like the anti-heroines of that American genre. She smokes a cigarette in a holder and makes suggestive remarks, while he continues trying to hang the wallpaper, to humorous effect:

> 'You're a nice-lookin' kid,' she said. 'Hasn't anybody told you that before?'
> 'Sure,' Mac said. 'What way would you like the frieze, Mrs. Ames?'
> 'Any way you like,' she said. 'So long as I get it.'

She asks him to call her Blondie – we have already been told that she has 'frizzy yellow hair', which sounds rather less glamorous – and rambles on about detectives and poison, while attempting to seduce Mac, who declines to play the role she has allotted him. There is something slightly sinister about the situation and Urquhart establishes a sense of tension, but the incongruity means that the story is mainly amusing. Perhaps *Tribune* published this story because it involves the unfair treatment of a worker.

The initial spark of the story, recorded in Urquhart's diary in September 1935, was also amusing. A young man who was papering and painting the Urquharts' living room told Urquhart's mother that a customer, who 'used to blether to him about her monkey-glands tablets', alarmed him 'one day when she gave him a cup of tea and passed the remark that it might be poisoned for all he knew. He says that he imagined he felt it taste funny and was all out in a sweat in case he dropped dead.' Elsewhere, Urquhart noted that he could write a story about the same woman 'always saying she thought [the painters] were Detectives'.[13]

'The Dream Book' also shows the influence of Hollywood on Scottish people – the typists try to model themselves on their favourite film stars, while the wisecracks exchanged by them and the junior clerk are imitating those in American comedies – but this element is not central to the story. It does, however, contribute to the rather infantile atmosphere – a symptom of class exploitation, perhaps – that Urquhart creates in the office where the young and innocent Betty works. The typists devotedly consult a book that supposedly interprets their dreams; Urquhart sends this up, when, for example, Betty dreams she 'was riding a horse through a field of ripe corn'. For Urquhart, horses always represent sexuality, not changing one's 'station in life', as *The Dream Book* suggests, while the 'ripe corn' is no doubt a comment on the banality of the dream and its interpretation.

Urquhart cleverly links Betty's confused sexual feelings towards the predatory Mr Miles with the latter's physical difference as a member of the upper-middle class; unlike her lower status boyfriend he is tall and well-built – he seems 'huge' to her – and not at all 'common-looking'. As a member of the working class himself, Urquhart was very conscious of such differences and the power they bestow. The workers in the office, as aspiring members of the middle class, do not use Scots, but a rather artificial and pretentious English (with references to 'the mater' and 'the pater', for example). Various details establish the Edinburgh middle-class milieu, particularly the fact that one of Betty's colleagues had been taken to 'the Pompadour Restaurant once when Anton Dolin was there': spotting a famous ballet dancer in a genuine leading restaurant – a perfect Edinburgh moment.[14] But there is a price to be paid for such things, as the ominous ending suggests.

This story was written earlier than the others in this collection, in February 1937, just after Urquhart had had a temporary job in the office of Grant's, an Edinburgh bookseller, where he was writing up the stock book. It was there that he had come across the real Dream Book: 'a relic of some typist . . . Every typist has consulted it on coming in in the morning. … Dickson [the manager] said that one typist had a dream about Baskets and it was so bad that she tore out the leaf.'[15]

The setting of 'But German Girls Walk Different' is Germany during the Occupation by the Allied forces following the end of the Second World War. The situation is in one way the reverse of 'The

Last G.I. Bride Wore Tartan', since the narrator is a working-class Scottish soldier who marries a German woman. His comrade Blister is Canadian, but he might as well be American, given his propensity to say things like 'We're gonna ride the range tonight! Yippee!' (It is also notable that it is an American soldier who provides the title of the story.) The narrator explains, in a convincing mixture of army slang and Glaswegian, how he acquires a German wife and horse, thanks to Blister's habit of 'winning', that is stealing things, particularly from the defeated Germans.

There are three typescripts of the story in Urquhart's papers. The original, with handwritten amendments, was begun in September 1945 (just four months after the end of the war in Europe) at Plymouth, where Urquhart was living with a sailor. It was completed on 7 January 1946 in Edinburgh, where Urquhart was staying at his parents' house after the end of the affair. The second typescript, marked '1st version' and typed out in Edinburgh shortly afterwards, contains some further amendments. The third is considerably cut down, with not just odd words removed to tighten sentences, but whole sections gone, including a grotesque account of Blister's habit of examining the teeth of mice before killing them. This typescript is almost identical to the text in this book, which tells the story in a much more economical and striking way than the earlier versions.

Urquhart deals with political issues that made the story appropriate for publication in *Tribune*, including the way in which the arrogance of officers from the upper classes encouraged soldiers to vote for Labour in the July 1945 general election and the policy of non-fraternisation, the ban on contact between the occupying British service personnel and German civilians. In the immediate aftermath of the war, the idea of a British soldier marrying a German was controversial; so much so that Urquhart noted that the advertised radio broadcast of this story on 27 February 1946 was 'cancelled by a B.B.C. director because he feared "Public opinion"'. He wrote, 'Got my 15 guineas fee, and that's all I care for.'[16] The B.B.C. eventually broadcast the story in September 1948.

The remaining two stories show little if any American influence. At the start of 'Hunt the Slipper', Sally, 'a respectable farmer's wife from Aberdeenshire', is queueing outside a shoe shop in the West End of London, not because there is a sale on, but because we are still in the years of continued rationing and shortages after the end of the Second World War. She has her eye on a 'frivolous' pair of sandals, blue with scarlet straps. Once inside the lavishly appointed shop, she is patronised by a 'disdainful' young assistant, who does not believe that Sally's feet are small enough to fit into the sandals. When Sally's charming male friend Terry arrives, the assistant's manner changes as she flirts with him.

One of the women in the queue had remarked, 'You can't tell these days ... Nobody ever is what they seem to be', and it is evident that Sally is actually a sophisticated and well-off woman (with small feet). (Urquhart may have had in mind his friend Jean Allan, the wife of John R. Allan, the Aberdeenshire farmer and writer.) That is evidently not how the assistant sees her, and Sally is aware that this will possibly be the case before she goes into the shop, thinking of herself as 'a country cousin' and worrying about possible embarrassments. She is also trying to moderate her Scottish accent (until she rebels).

The story is a study of an individual woman's psychology: Sally's eventual rebellion is possibly a reaction not only to the way she has been treated in the shop, but also to the fact that Terry does not see her as attractive in the way he sees the assistant. However, the story is also symbolic of the then relationship between Scotland and England, the former beset by feelings of inferiority vis-à-vis the latter, sure that its qualities will not be recognised, and ready to take offence, the latter disdainful and uninterested. Despite the fact that Urquhart disliked many aspects of Scotland, particularly the intolerance and bigotry that he experienced there (and the climate), he was always intensely aware, throughout his almost fifty years in England, that he was Scottish. (When the narrator of his story 'Dusty Springtime' [17] denies being English – '"British," I said, though I meant Scottish' – she speaks for him.)

The version of this story that appeared in *Woman's Own* [18] is shorter than the text here and removes most elements that might be controversial, such as the exclamation 'My God', the references to Terry being 'perverse', and Terry's remark that he 'might get off with one of the assistants', as well as his calling Sally 'ducky', a word that perhaps was not used by male characters in the magazine. It also reduces Sally's Scottishness: for example, her thinking that a woman may not understand her 'Aberdeen accent' is removed; Sally is made to say that she 'sometimes' takes size six-and-a half, not 'whiles'; and she doesn't ask for 'a wee shottie'. This weakens the national symbolism, but does not eliminate it. It is likely that the alterations were made at the magazine rather than by Urquhart.

'The Jolly Garçon' is set in an English village, where Miss Violet Ewart or Stubbings has retired to a windmill with her friend Miss Buchanan. Violet is looking for love, in the form of 'a strong silent man'. She becomes obsessed with a young soldier

– 'the Pretty Boy' – that the two women see in the local pub. He is in the company of a 'gipsy'; Miss Buchanan, as a 'wise and sophisticated Bohemian', assumes they are homosexual, like her young male friends in London. The two women do not speak to the soldier until the night the pub runs out of beer and cigarettes (another reminder of post-war shortages and rationing). The humour of the piece derives from the bitchy conversations of the two urban sophisticates and the revelation of their misreading of the local people, whom they have been too quick to stereotype.

Urquhart's female characters are usually completely convincing, but, when I first read this story, it was obvious to me that it is really about two gay men, one of whom wants to pick up a young man ('But you'd never look twice at him in Piccadilly, ducky.'). This was later confirmed to me by Urquhart, who said it was inspired by real events in the summer of 1946, when he and the Welsh writer Rhys Davies were sharing a rented cottage at Wigginton near Tring in Hertfordshire. The local pub was frequented by a young man they found attractive, so they called him the 'joli garçon'.[19] The rest of the story was largely invented, and the gender of the two main characters was, of necessity, disguised.

Seen in this light, a number of points take on extra meaning. Miss Buchanan, the Scotland-hating

Scottish writer (of romantic stories for women's magazines), who nevertheless sticks up for Scotland a couple of times, obviously stands for Urquhart, so Violet, despite being an actress and not apparently Welsh, must represent Davies. On 19 April 1947 Urquhart wrote in his diary, 'Rhys Davies used to say "This is a Black night" when things didn't go right at Wigginton.'[20] The words 'Black Night' are used by Violet three times when things go wrong. The pub name 'The Bugler's Call' could be a reference to Davies's young friend Colyn Davies, who was trained as a trumpeter in the army and provided the basis for Davies's story 'Boy with a Trumpet',[21] or, more generally, to Davies's and Urquhart's liking for soldiers. The pub landlord's surname was borrowed from an acquaintance of theirs. The reference to 'Arthur' and 'his guardsmen' could allude to Davies's brother, whose real first name was Arthur, although he was known as Peter, and the reference to young women taking drugs could relate to Davies's friend, the writer Anna Kavan. Like Miss Buchanan, Urquhart was addicted to cigarettes (at that time), and he too received fan-mail from readers of his women's magazine stories (including proposals of marriage).[22] When Miss Buchanan decides 'she'd have no more to do with psychological text-books', the joke is on Urquhart himself; Richard von Krafft-Ebing's *Psychopathia Sexualis* was an early influence on him. When Violet uses the words 'Different from the others' in relation to the Pretty Boy, it is presumably an allusion to the pro-gay German film *Anders als die Andern*. The return to London reflects the real-life failure of Urquhart's and Davies's attempt to live together in the country.[23]

When this book, Urquhart's fourth collection of stories, was first published, it received a wide range of generally favourable reviews. John Betjeman wrote, ' ... Fred Urquhart knows his women ... There is not a word wasted, not a sentence wrong.' [24] For John Pudney, Urquhart's 'specialities are good dialogue and bad women.'[25] It is true that Urquhart's women are particularly well drawn, although his men are also convincing; that his dialogue is so good that it creates living characters; and that his prose is expertly constructed. Added to his wit and humour, these qualities mean that this is still a very entertaining and enjoyable group of stories. But in addition, as *Tribune*'s reviewer stated, Urquhart's 'virtue ... is that he is essentially contemporary.'[26] This fact means that his work has historical as well as literary worth. Here he portrays – and allows the reader to bring back to life – various aspects of the first eighteen months or so of the postwar world. He also illustrates the strengthening of American cultural hegemony in the Britain of that era. The result is that these stories, in addition to their other merits, have the power to reveal people in a real past.

Colin Affleck

Notes

Documents in The Papers of Fred Urquhart in the Special Collections of Edinburgh University Library are indicated by 'EUL'. Other unpublished material is from Urquhart's personal archive.

1   Manuscript headed 'The Scent of Magnolia' and dated 12 August 1979.
2   Its first four books were published in 1947; Urquhart's was the fifth. Duncan Glen, *In Search of Serif Books, The Stanley Press and Joseph Mardel* (2006), p. 59.
3   Notes at back of notebook containing diary for 1940-48 (EUL MS 2827) and see correspondence with Forrester and Mardel.
4   'But German Girls Walk Different' and 'Call Me Blondie' first appeared in *Tribune* and 'Hunt the Slipper' in *Woman's Own* (which refused a version of 'The Dream Book').
5   Included in *The Year of the Short Corn (*1949), republished 2013.
6   James Drawbell, *Time on My Hands* (1968), p. 50. Another Scottish author whose work appeared in the magazine was Eric Linklater; see Drawbell's letter in *The Spectator* (28 February 1958), p. 16.
7   Report in *Woman's Own* (11 April 1947), pp. 10-11; Urquhart's manuscript notes about the party. In his autobiographical 'Forty Three Years: A Benediction', Urquhart describes laughing over 'The Last G.I. Bride Wore Tartan' with José Wilson: *The Ghost of Liberace (New Writing Scotland 11)* edited by A. L. Kennedy and Hamish Whyte (1993), p. 135.

8   Jenel Virden, *Good-bye Piccadilly: British War Brides in America* (1996), pp. 3, 64-5, 75, 88. Other sources have the ship's name as *Henry Gibbins*.
9   In real life the film producer Maurice Cowan took an option on making a film of this story, but unfortunately this came to nothing. Receipt dated 7 June 1948 for year's option on film rights.
10 Virden, p. 110.
11 In *The Clouds Are Big with Mercy* (1946), republished 2011.
12 Carbon copy of letter to J. S. Mardel, 26 August 1947.
13 Diary entry for 27 September 1935 (EUL MS 2826); note in notebook containing *Polish Your Brass*, etc.
14 In May 1936 Urquhart saw Dolin dancing as the Prince in an extract from *Swan Lake* at the King's Theatre in Edinburgh. He wrote in his diary: 'There's something devilish and cruel about him that I like. I wish I could meet him.' See also the reviews of the Markova-Dolin Ballet in *The Scotsman* of 9 and 16 May 1936.
15 Diary entries for 19 January and 8 and 10 February 1937 (EUL MS 2826); note in notebook containing *Polish Your Brass*, etc.
16 Notes at back of notebook containing diary for 1940-48 and diary entry for 27 February 1946 (EUL MS 2827).
17 Collected in *A Diver in China Seas* (1980), republished 2017.
18 Joint issue of 28 February and 7 and 14 March 1947.
19 Conversation with Urquhart, 13 August 1991. Some reviewers in 1948 apparently found the two women convincing: Allen Hutt in *The Daily Worker* (29 January 1948) wrote that '"The Jolly Garçon" [shows] with what skill he can pick off romantic ladies in early middle age', and P. H. Newby in *The New Statesman and Nation* (10 April 1948) described the plot of the story as 'two London ladies down in the country try to play Venus to a rustic Adonis'.

20 EUL MS 2827.
21 See Meic Stephens, *Rhys Davies: A Writer's Life* (2013), pp. 201-3. Urquhart's and Davies's co-tenancy is dealt with on pp. 224 and 233-5.
22 See 'Between Friends' in *Woman's Own* (joint issue of 28 February and 7 and 14 March 1947), p. 3.
23 Urquhart told me (on 26 November 1991) that the situation in another story, 'Luncheon Is Served' (included in his 1950 collection *The Last Sister*), was also based on the interlude in Wigginton. This story deals with a warring married couple in a 'tiny bungalow we'd taken for the summer' (although Urquhart and Davies were not a couple), and it includes references to the village of Pomfret Pond and The Bugler's Call, with its landlady, Mrs Dagnall.
24 *The Daily Herald*, 10 February 1948.
25 *Daily Express*, 2 February 1948.
26 *Tribune*, 20 February 1948.

THE LAST G.I. BRIDE WORE TARTAN

I

'I'M goin' to grab the last Yank in London,' I said.

We were standing at the top of the escalator in Piccadilly Circus Tube. My girl-friend, Violet, said: 'What's that? What're you muttering about, Jessie?'

But I didn't take time to answer. I grabbed her arm and cried: 'C'mon!' And I ran down the escalator ahead of her. I'd just seen an American soldier disappear down it, only his head and shoulders, like he was in a boat being carried over the Niagara Falls. It was only a glimpse, mind you, but it was enough. He was the first Yank I'd seen for weeks. Almost the first Yank I'd seen since I came to London. And I'd come to London to get a Yank. Honest to goodness I had. For months before I left Scotland, you could almost say for years, I'd thought about nothing else but getting a Yank. But there was no hope in a wee village like Birnieburn. All I could do was read about them in the papers. Every time I read about G.I. Brides I got real mad, wishing I was one of them. And when I got like that I read *Gentlemen Prefer Blondes* again and made up my mind that what Lorelei Lee did when she came to England I'd do when I got to the U.S.A. Only worse. Lorelei was going to have nothing on me. And so when finally I got round my mother to let me go to London to a job as a waitress in her second cousin's café I had really only one thing in mind: and that was to get a Yank.

The Last G.I. Bride Wore Tartan

But it wasn't as simple as all that. The War was over, and almost all the Yanks had gone home or had been sent to Occupied Germany. And those that were in London all had girl-friends already, who clung on to them like grim death and who'd have fought tooth and claw for them. I wasn't half mad, I can tell you, that the War hadn't lasted a bit longer. All the last year of it I kept hoping it would keep on long enough for me to be eighteen so that I could sort of say to my mother: 'Well, I guess it's time I went places and did things.' But it didn't; it stopped when I was seventeen years and seven months. And could I have wept!

But I didn't weep long. I put *Gentlemen Prefer Blondes* in a case along with my Stewart tartan skirt and my few other duds, and I went to London. The job in my second cousin's café wasn't so hot, but I chummed up with Violet, another waitress, and we went places.

This night we'd been to see Lauren Bacall's new film, and when I saw this American disappear down the escalator in Piccadilly Circus Tube I just rushed after him, because he was really the first American I'd seen by himself.

I was so excited I didn't wait to see if Violet was following. I rushed down two steps at a time.

It was all right for a minute. I could see him straight ahead of me. He wasn't walking; he was standing, leaning on the rail of the escalator. He had nice broad shoulders. And then for a few terrible seconds I couldn't see anything else. You see I'd forgotten that I'd been in London only a month and that I hadn't gotten used yet to the moving-staircases in the Tubes. At first I'd always stood on them, partly because I was terrified to walk down them and partly because I liked to get a good eyeful of the people who were travelling up the staircase

The Last G.I. Bride Wore Tartan

on the other side. But after the first week I plucked up courage and now I could walk up or down them all right and still watch the people.

That night, however, I was in such a panic when I saw this Yank I forgot I wasn't fully acclimatised and also that I was wearing pretty high heels. And so, before I knew properly where I was, I went head over heels and went rolling down the escalator.

They were a few terrible moments, I can tell you.

And then, before I knew where I was, there I was lying at the foot of the escalator and the Yank and two or three other people were bending over me. Away up above Violet was flying down, shouting: 'Oh, Jessie, are you hurt?'

Honest to goodness, I didn't know whether I was hurt or not. I was so surprised. But what I was most surprised at, I think, was the sight of the Yank's face.

He was no oil-painting.

II

'He wasn't worth taking a tumble for,' I said to Violet as soon as we were safely in our Tube. 'I wouldn't have had him with a pound of tea!'

'What did you want to follow him for anyway, love?' Violet said. 'You're crackers! Whatdja want a Yank for? All the best of them have been grabbed. Anyway, you wouldn't want to go away to America and leave all your friends, would you?'

'Chance me!' I said.

'Of course, I'd go like a shot,' I said. 'I want to go to Hollywood and get into pictures, and how'm I goin' to

The Last G.I. Bride Wore Tartan

get there if I don't get a Yank? How'm I goin' to pay the fare?'

Violet giggled. 'Ooooo, Jessie, wot things you say!'

'What's wrong with what I say?' I said. 'I'm hard. Hard. That's me!'

'Coo, but you ain't as hard as all that,' she said. 'You'd never marry a bloke, would you, then ditch him?'

'Whatdja think I'd do? Sit and twiddle my thumbs and watch him?' I laughed like I'd heard Hedy Lamarr laugh in a film when she was giving a bloke the run around. 'No, sister, not me! I'm gonna grab a Yank and get to America and then divorce him as sure as my name's Jessie M'Intyre.'

'Coo, but you *are* hard,' Violet said, and she looked at me as though I was the Statue of Liberty or something.

'You have to be hard in this world if you want to get on,' I said.

But I wasn't feeling as hard as I'd like to make out. I felt like crying. I'd hurt my knee when I fell and it was beginning to bother me. I was crippling a bit when we got out the Tube, and Violet got real worried.

'Let's take a taxi, love,' she said.

I said: 'Ach away, don't be daft, I can easy walk.' But before I could stop her she'd shot up her arm and yelled, and a taxi that was crawling past stopped.

'Number seven Mavisbloom Avenue,' Violet said, opening the door.

We'd just got in when the door opened again, and an American soldier jumped in. 'Sorry, girls,' he said, sitting down opposite us. 'But I sure had to get a cab and this was the only one in this God-forsaken bit of London. Which way you goin'?'

'Well, of all the cheek!' Violet said.

The Last G.I. Bride Wore Tartan

I couldn't say anything. For a moment I thought it was the Yank on the escalator who'd followed us, but then I realised it wasn't; this guy had the same kind of broad shoulders, but that was all they had in common. This guy was a perfect picture.

'Listen you,' Violet said. 'We don't want to share this taxi with anybody, so you'd better skedaddle—and skedaddle quick!'

'Aw, have a heart, sister,' the Yank said. 'I want to get to a place pretty damn quick, and if I drop you girls first it'll be quicker than waiting for another cab. See my point?'

'I see nothing,' Violet said. 'Except the shine on your brass neck. It's blindin' me.'

'Aw, nuts!' he said.

'Look, I'll pay for the cab,' he said. 'After I drop you dames. . . .'

'Listen, brother,' Violet said. 'Whatdja think we are? You get out of here pretty quick or I'll tell the driver to stop and call a policeman. Don't you know it's illegal to share a taxi?'

'Aw look, baby!' he said.

The taxi had stopped at some traffic lights and they were shining right in full on him. He was leaning forward, grinning. Honest to goodness, I must say he looked good. But I was determined to be on my high-horse the same as Violet.

'My girl-friend has asked you to go,' I said as icy as I could. 'So please do so. No gentleman would stay where he wasn't wanted.'

'But I ain't no gentleman, baby,' he said, laughing. 'I'm just a simple guy from the Middle West. Name's Lew Winnegar. What's yours?'

'Come, Violet,' I said. 'We'll just ask the driver to

The Last G.I. Bride Wore Tartan

drop us here. We can easy walk the rest. Since this gentleman's in such a hurry that he's forgotten his manners we might as well show him that at least *we've* been well brought up.'

'But your leg, ducks!' Violet cried. 'You can't walk with it.'

'I'll do my best,' I said on my dignity. 'I think I'll be able to bear the pain. Anyway, to-morrow's my day off, so I can rest then.'

'Look, sister,' the Yank said. 'I don't want to bother you, honest I don't. But I simply gotta be at this place by a certain time, and cabs are mighty difficult to get. Have a heart. Please!'

'Have a heart yourself,' Violet said. 'Think of my girl-friend's leg.'

'Which she hurt through the fault of another American soldier,' she said with a snap.

'Well, we haven't far to go now,' I said, musing like. 'I daresay we can let you share it. . . .'

'Say, that's swell!' he cried. 'You're a coupla peaches and I'm mighty. . . .'

'But kindly don't talk to us,' I said, leaning as far back as I could in my corner. 'We aren't interested.'

I could see we were getting near Mavisbloom Avenue. Violet was getting all ready to say something, but I gave her a dig and she shut up. The Yankee started to say something, too, but he gave it up. We drove the last few minutes in silence.

The taxi stopped and me and Violet got out. Violet leaned in to pay the driver, but before she could say anything the Yank said: 'Okay, driver, make it the one fare. Drive me now to Grosvenor Square. Goodnight, girls, thanks a lot!'

And before we could say anything the taxi drove off.

The Last G.I. Bride Wore Tartan

Violet and me just stood and looked at each other. 'Well, of all the cool cheek,' Violet said as soon as she'd got her breath. 'He might at least have stopped long enough to thank us properly. I thought we'd got off with him.'

'So did I,' I said.

III

The next morning when I was reading *Gentlemen Prefer Blondes* for the sixteenth time and wondering what new wrinkles I could get, Mrs. Percy, the landlady, knocked on the door. 'This just came by taxi,' she said, handing in a large cardboard box.

It was addressed to 'The Young Lady in the Tartan Skirt.'

It was full of carnations that must have cost a fortune, and on top of them was a card: 'Will you meet me at three o'clock in the Café Lenore in Shaftesbury Avenue and I'll apologise for last night? Lew Winnegar.'

'What a cheek!' I said.

At ten-past three when I went into the Café Lenore he was sitting at a table near the door. He jumped up and pulled out a chair. 'Park yourself, sis,' he said.

'Good afternoon,' I said on my dignity.

But he wasn't the kind that could be frozen. He was even nicer in the daylight than I'd thought. He had pale grey eyes that looked even paler because of the thick fringe of black eyelashes. Like lots of Americans I'd seen he looked as if he'd been poured into his uniform. It was kind of tight across the seat. But for all that he was all right.

In less than a week he was my steady fella. I was a

The Last G.I. Bride Wore Tartan

G.I.'s moll like I'd always wanted to be. And in less than a fortnight I was a G.I. Bride. And so I quit work and settled down to live on my allowance, and when Lew was sent back to Germany I had a rare old time, gadding around London.

I got a right kick out of writing home and telling my mother I was a married woman now and that I was all set to sail for the U.S.A. as soon as the authorities could arrange my passage. And I got a bigger kick when I was able to go home to Birnieburn for a couple of weeks and show off all the new clothes Lew had bought me. My mother was a bit flabbergasted when she saw them and she said: 'But where did ye get all the coupons, Jessie?'

'The black market,' I said. 'Lew paid two bob a coupon. He bought about eighty.'

'Lord preserve us, Jessie M'Intyre,' my mother said. 'Ye were daft to let him spend all that money on ye. My word, if I'd been in London beside ye I'd have put my foot down good and hard. The clothes ye had already were fine; ye werenie needin' new ones.'

'Aw, nuts!' I said.

'I'll aw nuts ye!' she said. 'Maybe ye're a married woman now, but that'll no' prevent me frae gi'en ye a scud on the jaw if I have any more o' yer impiddence.'

So I said 'Aw nuts!' to myself this time. I was hard put to it to keep my temper that fortnight I was at home, for my mother found fault with everything. She was right rattled that I was going away to the States where she wouldn't be able to come into my house when I got one and tell me how to run it. 'I just hope yer man's mother is a sensible body,' she said. 'I hope she'll keep her weather-eye on ye and see that ye feed him right and that ye don't get led away wi' too many o' yer daft notions.' She kept weeping every now and then, saying:

The Last G.I. Bride Wore Tartan

'It's such a long way to Americky. Yer puir faither and me'll never be able to afford the fare to come and visit ye, so it's hardly likely we'll ever see ye again in this world.'

'And not in the next if I can help it,' I said to myself. My mother gives me a pain.

So I was right glad when I got a telegram from Lew to say he'd left Germany and was coming to London on his way back to the U.S.A. And so I got on the first train and said good-bye to Birnieburn and all the folks without much regret. At least I thought I did, and you can imagine how annoyed I was, just after my mother and father had seen me off in the train at Dundee, when I had to go to the toilet in case I burst into tears in the compartment before a lot of strangers.

Lew was in London only two days before he sailed for New York, so we made hay. The last night he was like a kid: almost blubbering. 'I hate to go and leave you, Jessie,' he said. 'I'll be countin' the days until you come and join me in Struthers Bridge, Minnesota.'

'Ach away!' I said.

'I sure got a case on you, babe,' he said.

'Ach away!' I said.

'Honest,' he said.

'Ach away!' I said. 'I don't believe you.'

All the same I wept buckets when we said good-bye, and as soon as he'd gone I made a bee-line for the American Embassy to see how soon it'd be before I got a passage. They were awful nice, and so were the people at the shipping company. They all said they'd give me a passage as soon as they could, and they gave me a booklet called *A Bride's Guide To The U.S.A.* and they told me to go home and study it and to content myself.

But I practically parked myself on their doorsteps for the next few weeks, and while I waited for visas and all

The Last G.I. Bride Wore Tartan

the other things I read *Gentlemen Prefer Blondes* and this booklet time about. And the tips in this booklet were right funny, I can tell you. By the time I'd read it two three times I felt I knew America from top to bottom. And so I was real glad when there was a phone call to say another G.I. Bride had fallen ill and would I like to take her passage on a boat. I didn't stop to wonder what had happened to this dame; I collected my duds and got on the first train for Southampton. I was on my way to America at last, and 'California, Here I Come!' was my theme-song.

IV

There were a lot of G.I. Brides on the boat. I shared a cabin with three others. They were all older than me and because they'd been married longer and had gone with lots of Yanks they ribbed me no end. They were a bit snooty about my clothes, so I sure had a nice time with them.

'Why d'you always wear that old tartan skirt, Scotty?' Isobel said. 'Haven't you got any other clothes?'

'Sure,' I said. 'I've got a lot of clothes, but they're all in the hold in my trunks marked "Not Wanted on the Voyage."'

'That's not gonna do you much good,' Letty said, fixing her face in front of the mirror for about the nineteenth time that day.

'Well, they won't wear out there,' I said.

'Proper Scotty, aren't you!' Isobel laughed. 'Whatya mean keepin' them for, kid? Your grandchildren, etc., etc.?'

'No,' I said. 'But it says in the *G.I. Bride's Guide* that

The Last G.I. Bride Wore Tartan

you should dress smartly for first interviews, so I'm keepin' them for that.'

'D'ya expect your mother-in-law to give you the once-over before she lets you share a room with her blue-eyed boy?' Cora said.

'Nuts for my mother-in-law!' I said. 'I'm keepin' them till I get to Hollywood.'

'But you ain't goin' as far as Hollywood,' Isobel said. 'Where's your knowledge of geography? If you'd read your *G.I. Bride's Guide* carefully you'd see that a knowledge of American geography is necessary before you can become an American citizen. You aren't likely to make the grade if you don't know that Struthers Bridge, Minnesota, is sixteen hundred miles north east of Hollywood, etc., etc.'

'I do so know that,' I said. 'But all the same I'm goin' to Hollywood some time—and not before too long either!'

'Hubby gonna take you there?' Cora asked.

'Not on your life!' I said. 'I'm goin' myself. I'm gonna go into films.'

'Greta MacGarbo the second!' Letty giggled.

'Ach, you can laugh if you like,' I said. 'But I'm goin'. What do ye think I'm goin' to America for? Do ye think I grabbed a G.I. just so's I could settle down in a wee house in the Middle West? Not on your lives! I'm a lot harder than you dames seem to think.'

'Well, I must say, Scotty, it shows a very nasty spirit,' Isobel said. 'I don't know what's comin' over the girls nowadays.'

'G.I.'s,' Cora said.

'I'd never dream of leading a guy up the garden like that,' Isobel said. 'Mind you, I'm no angel myself, but I always believe in putting my cards on the table, etc., etc.

The Last G.I. Bride Wore Tartan

I'd never of dreamt of marryin' my Mervyn if I hadn't been in love with him hook, line and sinker.'

'Nor me,' Cora said. 'My Alvin would strangle me if he thought I was goin' to America just to go on the movies.'

'Well, Lew'll just have to make the best of it,' I said. 'I told him before I married him that I was hard. If he won't let me go to Hollywood to see what I can do, then he can just divorce me. I won't mind.'

'That's not the proper spirit, Scotty,' Isobel said. 'And speaking of spirit—what about a little snifter, girls?'

When she came aboard Isobel had six bottles of whisky and gin that she'd brought with her from Germany, where she'd had a job with the Allied Control Commission. Her loot, she called it. She said she was keeping it until she got to North Dakota so that she and Mervyn could celebrate their reunion. But before we'd been long on the voyage she opened the first bottle, saying: 'One bottle less won't mean a thing to Mervyn, and us girls certainly need it to keep up our morale, etc., etc.'

She said the same about the second bottle, and about the third. By the time she'd opened the fourth bottle she'd forgotten about it, though.

'Well, here's to us all!' she said now.

And so then Cora took out her loot. She had boxes and boxes of hundreds and hundreds of cigarettes. She was right mean about them and whenever she left an open box lying around she dusted the fags with black powder so that she'd see if anybody had been tampering with them.

But that night she was all hail-fellow-well-met and come-hither-and-take-a-fag. And so the rest of us weren't slow in coming forward.

The Last G.I. Bride Wore Tartan

'I'm just crazy to get to Rhode Island,' Cora said after a while. 'I'm just crazy to see my Alvin again.'

'You're crazy enough already,' Letty said.

'That's an obvious wisecrack,' Isobel said. 'You shouldn't be obvious in this world. Now Scotty here is far, far too obvious. If she acts like she's doing, her hubby and his people will chuck her out neck and crop before she's been with them a week.'

'And serve her right too,' Cora said. 'It's not nice of Scotty to act so gold-diggerish, like the dame in that book she's always reading. I'd be ashamed to act like her.'

'Not that I need to,' she said, taking another drink. 'Because I adore my Alvin. I'm just crazy about my Alvin.'

'I'm crazy about my fella too,' Letty said, going to the mirror and taking another decka at herself. 'I'll always remember the first night I met Bill. I heard the Wolf Call and I answered it.'

'Well, I didn't hear any Wolf Call,' I said. 'Lew barged into the taxi I was in, and I was right annoyed, I can tell you.'

'I know another girl who met her G.I. in a taxi,' Isobel said, pouring out more drinks. 'She went to his people in Arkansas last year, and was it a flop! Do you know, they lived in a shack beside the railway, where they sold snacks to the railwaymen. This friend of mine was proper peeved, etc., etc. After him telling her he owned a chain of restaurants!'

'My Alvin would never do anything so mean as that to me,' Cora said, taking another swig. 'He's on the level, my Alvin is. He's a partner in a firm of solicitors in Providence, R.I., and he's got a swell apartment waiting for me.'

Cora was all prepared to launch out into another

The Last G.I. Bride Wore Tartan

description of this apartment, so I said: 'Did I show you the cartoon my mother sent me from a paper?' And I rummaged in my bag and found it and passed it round. It certainly was a right take-off on all the G.I. Bride stories. It showed a G.I. and his Bride and their kid arriving at his old homestead, a terrible shack in the backwoods, with all his family lying around in rags. They were all smoking pipes, from the old granny in her rocking-chair to the wee baby playing in the dust without any clothes on. I had thought it right funny when my mother sent it, though I hadn't been so pleased at what she'd written on the back. 'Be Warned!'

The girls passed it from one to another, and they all laughed, but nobody said anything. Then Cora said: 'What about gettin' another station on the radio? Somethin' lively. I'm tired of this "Drink to me only with thine eyes" stuff. Let's have "Beat Me, Daddy, with a Bottle of Gin." That's what I call Life!'

But we couldn't find anything lively, so we had some more drinks, and then Isobel began to tell us about one seventy-two-hours' leave she'd had in Berlin and about the juicy experiences she'd had. And she got fairly going about some fella she'd met on a train who'd taken her around the night clubs and how they'd sat up almost all night drinking in an hotel. But I didn't listen much to her, I kept looking at this G.I. Bride cartoon and thinking about Lew, who after all was more or less a stranger.

V

The night before the boat docked there was a dance aboard. There was a right kick-up in our cabin while we got ready for it. Letty would have hogged the mirror

The Last G.I. Bride Wore Tartan

all the time, 'lashing herself up', as she called it, but we weren't having any.

'Get away from that mirror, you,' Isobel said. 'Give us a chance to get lashed up, too.'

'It would take a lot of lashing,' Letty said, without moving. 'Especially Scotty there! She looks out of this world in that get-up.'

'What's wrong with my get-up?' I said.

'Nothing, dear, nothing,' Isobel said quickly. 'I'm sure it was a very nice frock and in the height of fashion in nineteen-thirty-nine.'

'Ach, go and fry your face!' I said, because I couldn't think of anything else to say. But I was real mad, and I wished I'd never been such a fool as to listen to Violet when she told me not to wear my best duds on the voyage. But I was determined I'd show them as soon as I got to New York. And when I got to Hollywood—well, they'd laugh on the other side of their faces when they saw me on the movies, looking like a couple of million dollars. They'd just be plain American housewives by that time, going to the movies once a week regular as clockwork; and it was nice to think of them sitting back in their seats, saying: 'Gee, I came across in the same boat as that dame. She's gone places since then.'

Anyway, I didn't see anything wrong with my pale blue organdie. It had been good enough for the Hammersmith Palais de Danse, where I'd had my moments even after I married Lew. So I reckoned it was good enough for an old dance on a tub like this.

I was right. We weren't five minutes in the ballroom before a fella came up and asked me to dance. I wasn't surprised at this, but the other dames were. Because this was an awful high-hat sort of fella called Paul Whittaker

The Last G.I. Bride Wore Tartan

that all the dames had been trying to make ever since the boat sailed. He was a journalist or something, going to the States on a lecture tour. He was a real smasher, so I gave the girls the wink as I fox-trotted away with him.

I knew a lot of gen about Paul already, because news travels fast aboard ship, but while we danced and then after while we sat the next one out, he told me a lot more. He was a pretty high-up guy in the newspaper world, it seemed, and he knew everybody it was worth knowing. So I told him a few things about myself and about how I aimed to go to Hollywood, because I figured maybe he might have contacts there which would come in handy when the time came.

By the time the dance was half-way through Paul was all over me, but I was keeping a grip of myself. I was kind of attracted, mind you, for he was tall and he had a nice pink and white face that I wouldn't have minded smoothing over with my hands. And his close-cropped golden hair just shouted out to be touched. But I kept telling myself I was a married woman and that the next day Lew would be waiting on the dock for me. Though it was awful difficult, because I hadn't had such a good time with a fella for quite a long time.

And so when he said to come up on deck for a breather I went like a shot, but telling myself to watch my step. And I watched it all right, too, though he drew me into a dark corner beside one of the life-boats and put his arm round my waist.

'You're far too young to be married, Jessie,' he said. 'A girl like you should have a good time before you settle down to married life.'

'I can still have a good time and be married,' I said. 'I don't see why gettin' married should make any difference.'

The Last G.I. Bride Wore Tartan

'That's what *you* think,' he said. 'But what would your husband's views be?'

'Ach, if he doesn't like it he can lump it,' I said. 'I told him before I married him that I was out to have a good time and that I wasn't prepared to settle down into a housewife for a long time yet.'

'You talk hard, Jessie,' he said, and he gave a bit laugh. 'But really you're a nice girl underneath, aren't you? Come on, own up!'

'I'm not a nice girl at all,' I said.

'Ah, but you are,' he said. 'If you weren't you'd have proved it to me already.'

I didn't say anything to this, because I was trying to figure how Lorelei Lee would have acted in the same situation.

'I knew you were a nice girl as soon as I set eyes on you,' Paul said. 'The funny thing is that as a rule I don't like nice girls. They bore me to tears. But you're different.'

'Ach away!' I said.

'Yes, you are,' he said. 'I don't think I've ever met anybody quite like you—and I've known lots of girls in my time. But the odd thing is that I've never met one I'd rather be with than you.'

'Ach away!' I said, and I was so busy trying to think of something else to come-back with that I didn't make any move when he put his arm a bit tighter round me. It was real pleasant to stand there in the darkness close to him, with the moon shining on the ripples of the sea far away below us.

I don't know how long we'd have stood like this, and I don't think we'd have gone any further, but just then somebody giggled beside us, and Isobel said: 'Don't make yourself cheap, ducky!'

The Last G.I. Bride Wore Tartan

And so for spite I reached up and kissed Paul right before the eyes of Isobel and Cora and Letty. I was right mad at them. They had no call to come and butt in like this just because they were jealous.

But Paul took away his arm. 'What about you and your friends coming for a drink?' he said.

'That would be swell,' Isobel said, and she put her arm through his.

We were moving towards the cocktail bar when a steward went past shouting: 'Everybody in ballroom, please! Everybody in ballroom. The captain has an important announcement to make. . . .'

VI

When we got into the ballroom the Captain was standing on his hind-legs on the platform beside the band, but he was waiting for everybody to come in before he said his little piece. We all stood around, wondering what it could be about, and there were lots of speculations. Some of the dames had the wind up, saying they were sure we'd struck an iceberg or something disastrous. But I knew we hadn't felt any jolt, and so I was right amused at them saying: 'Maybe this is going to be another *Lusitania*.'

At least, I would have been amused if I hadn't been so annoyed at Isobel and Co. butting in the way they'd done. It wasn't that I was so desperately keen on Paul, but I hadn't had a man put his arms round me and kiss me for at least a fortnight, and so I was real burnt-up. I tried to edge him through the crowd, away from Isobel and the others, and when I'd manœuvred this I said: 'I'm afraid my girl-friends were a bit rude just now.'

The Last G.I. Bride Wore Tartan

'One picks one's own friends,' he said, kind of distant like.

'Well, I didn't pick these,' I said. 'The shipping company picked them for me.'

'Anyway,' I said, 'one isn't to blame for what one's friends say.'

'Possibly not,' he said, but he kept that frozen look on his face and he never made any more moves to be friendly.

I was just figuring out what I'd do when the Captain held up his hand for silence and said:

'Ladies and Gentlemen—and G.I. Brides!'

He paused for a laugh, and of course he got one.

'I have a very important announcement to make,' he said. 'As you are all aware—indeed how could we possibly be unaware of the presence of so many charming young ladies—there are a number of G.I. Brides on this ship. To be exact there are ninety-seven of them. Ninety-seven charming young women who are on the threshold of attaining American citizenship. Let's all give them a big hand!'

And so while everybody cheered and clapped, us G.I. Brides stood and tried to look as if butter wouldn't melt in our mouths—and I must say it must have been a difficult job for some of those dames. But I knew I didn't need to pretend to look starry-eyed and simple.

'Now as you know,' the Captain continued, 'the United States Government has sponsored the voyages of these charming young ladies to their new homes in this great country. But unfortunately the United States Government do not feel that they can go on doing this indefinitely, and so they have decided that the last official G.I. Bride is sailing on this ship. Of course, there will still be a great many more G.I. Brides coming across

The Last G.I. Bride Wore Tartan

the Atlantic, we hope, but these young ladies will have to come without official sponsoring. That does not mean that they won't be welcomed with open arms by Uncle Sam and his boys—especially his boys!'

He stopped for another laugh and took a drink of water or something.

'But this ship is carrying the last official G.I. Bride,' he said. 'And now my problem is to say which of you ninety-seven lovely young ladies is that privileged person. It is a hard task. A far harder task than a poor weak male like myself cares to tackle! But the United States Government has given me an order, and so as a loyal simple-minded seaman I am going to do my best to carry out this order.'

He paused while everybody whispered and looked at each other. And we were all on tiptoe when a couple of stewards propelled a huge barrel on to the platform and set it end up beside the Captain.

'I've wracked my brains as to which is the best way to solve this problem,' the Captain said. 'At first I thought I would make the youngest bride on board the last official bride, but I came to the conclusion that this wouldn't do. I didn't fancy asking all these ninety-seven young ladies to produce their birth certificates. I felt it would be unchivalrous! And so I've thought of another way out. In this barrel there are ninety-seven envelopes. Each envelope is sealed. Inside each is a slip of paper with a number. I must now ask all the G.I. Brides to line up and come forward and take an envelope from the barrel, and I must also ask them to wait until I give the word before she breaks open her envelope.'

There was a lot of giggling and pushing as we all lined up, and everybody was doing her best to look coy. Isobel and Cora and Letty and me were well at the head

The Last G.I. Bride Wore Tartan

of the queue, I can tell you, and we all blushed like nobody's business as we got up on the platform and took an envelope from the barrel.

I was just itching to rip my envelope open, but of course none of us dared do it until the Captain gave the word. We were all wondering what number we'd got—not that it mattered much as he hadn't said which number was the right one—and we all kept holding them up to the light to see if we could see. But the envelopes were pretty thick and we could see nothing.

'Now,' the Captain said, when the last dame had taken her envelope, 'now that you have all got your envelopes, I wish you to open them, and then I want the young lady who has the number ninety-seven to step up here. She is the last official G.I. Bride!'

VII

There was such a ripping open of envelopes as you never saw. Not that I saw much of it; I just heard the rustle. I was too busy ripping open my own envelope.

I had the number ninety-seven!

Of course, I could have told that before the envelope was open, long before the last dame had dipped into the barrel, because every girl knows that she has got the lucky number. All the same you could have knocked me down with a feather, and my knees were shaking so much I could hardly get up on the platform.

I was still in a daze when the Captain took my hand and shouted: 'Ladies and Gentlemen, may I present—the last official G.I. Bride!'

'What's your name, dear?' he whispered.

The Last G.I. Bride Wore Tartan

I tried to whisper it back, but I could hardly make my lips move and I had to say it twice before he got it.

'Ladies and Gentlemen,' he cried. 'Allow me to present Mrs Jessie Winnegar!'

After a lot of clapping and cheering lots of people cried: 'Speech! Speech!' But I hung back, and the Captain said: 'The little lady's shy, so we mustn't embarrass her more than we can help. Let me just greet her in my official capacity, and welcome the last G.I. Bride.'

Then he kissed me on the cheek in quite a fatherly way.

'I think,' he said, 'that if I'd carried out my original plan of asking all these young ladies to show their birth certificates in order to find the youngest, Mrs Winnegar would still have been chosen, so you other young ladies mustn't be disappointed that you didn't pick the lucky number.'

'I'm right, my dear, amn't I?' he said to me. 'How old are you?'

'Eighteen,' I whispered.

'There you are!' he cried. 'I was right. Mrs Winnegar is only eighteen. Am I right in thinking that none of you other young ladies are *quite* so young as that?'

There was a lot more laughing and clapping, but I saw some of the other brides looking real mad at me. However, I didn't mind. The Captain was holding my hand in a right nice and fatherly way, and I felt safe standing beside him.

I was still feeling so good after the dance finished that when I went back to our cabin I was singing: 'I'm the last of the Red Hot Mommas.'

'Positively the last, ducky,' Isobel said in a catty way. 'But you'll cool down quick enough, too, when you get to that little hick town in the Middle West. It won't

[*34*]

The Last G.I. Bride Wore Tartan

be long before you're singing "Don't Fence Me In," etc. etc.'

VIII

The next morning passed in a daze. There was all the excitement of seeing the Statue of Liberty and the New York skyline, and then getting ready to disembark. And then an official party came on board, the Mayor of New York and a lot more officials, and before I knew where I was they were greeting me like a long-lost sister, telling me the whole city was mine. I was fair away with myself, and I didn't mind the photographers and the radio guys with microphones at all. I wasn't in the least little bit shy. The funny thing was that I didn't mind a bit not having got my new clothes out of the hold, because everybody admired my tartan skirt. I fair enjoyed myself, and so did Isobel and Cora and Letty, for they hadn't been long in announcing they were my buddies and horning in on the photographers and the radio. I'll never forget Isobel saying in an awful posh tone into a microphone: 'I am ever so pleased to come to America and I am sure that my life here will be ever so happy. I am looking forward ever so much to becoming an American citizen, and I am sure my little friend, Jessie Winnegar, is too. Jessie is a very nice girl and I am ever so glad that she has been chosen to be the last official G.I. Bride. But I'm even more glad that we are to be near neighbours in this great country. On the steamer coming over she was a familiar sight in her tartan skirt, and I am sure that you will all love her as much as we do. Once you can understand her Scotch accent Jessie is a very, very nice girl and ever so sweet, and I am looking forward to going to visit her in her new

The Last G.I. Bride Wore Tartan

home at Struthers Bridge, Minnesota, after we've both settled down to becoming American housewives, etc. etc.'

I couldn't help giggling at Isobel saying 'etc. etc.' even when she was at the mike, though I was annoyed at her hogging it so much when all the radio guys had done had been to ask her to introduce me. But I didn't get time to think of all this because one of the guys waved me forward and there I was!

I don't know what I said, but I guess I managed all right. I only said a few words, and I stammered most of them. I clean forgot about what the *G.I. Bride's Guide* said about trying to retain your own accent because Americans like it. I wish I'd remembered and put in a few 'Ochs' and rolled my *r*s for good measure, but you can't think of these things at the time. I did remember what I'd seen Carole Lombard do in a film, but I was too scared to do it. I wonder what would have happened if I'd said: 'Are ye listenin', Ma? This is yer wee lassie speaking all the way from America. I hope ye're well, Ma. I'm all right. Ta, ta, Ma!'

But even if I'd said it I guess my mother wouldn't have heard it because she would be at the wash-tub at the time, and anyway she wasn't likely to be listening to an American radio station. Still, it's a pity I didn't do it, because they might have put headlines like TARTAN-CLAD G.I. BRIDE SAYS HELLO TO HER MOTHER IN SCOTLAND, instead of putting things like TARTAN-CLAD G.I. BRIDE HAS MIKE FRIGHT.

And the next thing was Lew was there, kissing me right in front of everybody with the cameras going nineteen to the dozen. And Cora's Alvin was there, too, and so was Letty's Bill. But Isobel's Mervyn couldn't come all that distance from North Dakota—though Lew

The Last G.I. Bride Wore Tartan

had come just as far for me. Still, she tagged along, and the seven of us went places and did things in New York that evening, and for several days after that. And I must say Isobel being with us was a right nuisance, because she kept making up to Lew. In a way I don't blame her, for he was the swellest-looking guy of them all, but I got real mad sometimes when she clung on to his arm and kept treating him like he was her property. Personally I wouldn't have given two dimes for Cora's Alvin, and why she'd made all the song and dance about him is beyond me. He was as thin as a pole and about six feet four. Cora herself was about five feet ten, which made Isobel say to me: 'Goodness knows what their kids'll be like! Six feet six at least! It'll be kinda hard on the girls, if they have any!' There was one good thing about it all, though. Letty discovered the Du Barry Beauty Salon and she was never out of it, so that left her Bill free, and Isobel was able to hitch on to him sometimes. Though if I'd been as soft as I look she'd have had me tag along with him while she monopolised my Lew.

Isobel is all right, and I quite like her, but I must say I was glad when Lew and I said good-bye to her at St. Paul. We'd had her company all the way on the train and I was a bit sick of it. We clung to each other and kissed, and Isobel said: 'You'll keep in touch, won't you, Scotty? We'll always be friends, won't we?' And I said: 'Sure, sure, I'll always remember you, Isobel.' Though I didn't mean this in the way she meant. I was thankful that Rivers End, North Dakota, was a tidy step from Struthers Bridge, so I thought I was safe in saying: 'We'll see each other soon,' as we waved good-bye.

And so you'll know how I felt when she appeared on my front porch a week ago, saying: 'Honey, I've left my husband. Can you put me up until I make my plans?'

The Last G.I. Bride Wore Tartan

IX

Of course, a lot of water had flowed under the bridge in the month before this happened, so I'd better put it all down first.

Lew had told me Struthers Bridge was quite a small place and that his father owned the main store. Lew worked in this store and until we got a home of our own we were to live with his parents. 'You'll like my Mom,' he said. 'She's swell. You'll like my Pop, too. He's looking forward to meeting his new daughter-in-law.'

I was kind of nervous, hoping it wouldn't turn out to be a wee place like Birnieburn—though I told myself even if it did I wouldn't be there such a long time, after all, because pretty soon I'd be lighting out for Hollywood.

But it turned out to be a fairly decent-sized place, and it even has a cinema. We're only twenty-five miles from St. Paul and we go there whenever we want to hit the high spots. Lew likes to go places as much as I do. He says Struthers Bridge is kind of cramping after being in the Army.

Pop Winnegar's store is quite large, almost as big as a Woolworth's in Perth or Dundee. I'd been picturing Lew in a white apron serving behind the counter, but it turns out that he sits in a small office dealing with accounts and running the business for his Pop, who has more or less retired now that Lew has quit soldiering. This makes Lew a pretty important guy in Struthers Bridge; the Winnegars are pretty important people, and Pop has been Mayor of the place for years and years.

But in a way Pop being retired is right wearing for me. Because he spends a lot of time at home, sitting on the front porch or fiddling around with the radio. I reckon

The Last G.I. Bride Wore Tartan

I've enough to deal with when I've got Mom Winnegar at my tail all day without having the old man always butting in, too.

Mom Winnegar is tall and thin, with a florid complexion. She is very dignified and what she calls better-class. According to her there are three grades: no class, better class and class. She is too much of a lady to say which grade she belongs to, but I know she reckons she is class in Struthers Bridge, but only better-class in big places like St. Paul and New York. She is a great one for the Social Register. She wears toques like Queen Mary, only they are usually black or dark brown. She says her admiration for the Queen Mother has gone down in recent years because she keeps on wearing pastel shades. 'I reckon it ain't dignified for a lady of her age to wear such light colours,' she told me. She asked if I'd seen the King and Queen close, and when I said I'd never seen them at all she said: 'My land, if I lived in London I'd just hang around Buckingham Palace and hang around until I saw them.'

'I reckon you should study the pictures of Princess Elizabeth, Jessie,' she said. 'You'd be well advised to take a leaf out of her book when it comes to dress. She's got class.'

But I turn a deaf ear when she says this, because when it comes to dress I don't need anybody to tell me what's what. And anyway, if I felt the need to study anybody I'd rather study Ginger Rogers or Betty Grable. I know what suits me. I guess it's a pity Mom Winnegar doesn't. She should take a decka at herself sometimes in those dark-coloured toques.

So it isn't so hot living with Lew's people, but I guess I could bear that all right. What gets my goat most is the various old friends of the family who are always

The Last G.I. Bride Wore Tartan

dropping in or asking us to visit them. It's not my idea of pleasure to go and sit on somebody's porch in the evening and listen to two three old people about seventy talking about the weather and each other's ailments. And it's not Lew's idea either, thank goodness. Like me, he likes nothing better than to get into the automobile and head for St. Paul. There have been quite a few rumpuses about this, especially nights when Mom Winnegar has invited people over for coffee and cakes and me and Lew have lit out. She never says a great deal about it at the time, but sooner or later she drops something out about: 'Of course, Lew ain't his Mom's baby any more. Poor Mom'll have to remember that her baby's got a wife who takes first place.'

The first week I was here Mom Winnegar spent a lot of time quizzing me about my ancestors and about Birnieburn. I had to tell her where exactly it was, how many miles from Perth and how many miles from Dundee. She got out an atlas and looked up the map of Scotland, following all the details. And she got fair excited and said: 'My land, you must come from right near the place where old Mr. Neill's grandfather came from.' And nothing would stop her until she'd asked this old Mr. Neill along one evening for coffee and cakes, to meet me. It appeared that Mr. Neill's father and Mom's mother had been brought up in places right near each other in Pennsylvania, but otherwise they had nothing in common because he had been what she called 'a no account cattle thief.'

Still, she asked him along one evening, and it was right boring for me and Lew, because Mom made me wear my tartan skirt, and we all sat there on the porch while old Mr. Neill spoke about some book called *The Bonnie Briar Bush* and about his clan and his clan's tartan. 'I'm

The Last G.I. Bride Wore Tartan

seventy-seven,' he said. 'But there's life in the old hoss yet, young lady. And one of these days I aim to make the trip and see the land of my fathers.'

All I can say is the quicker he makes this trip and gets away from Struthers Bridge the better I'll like it. I sure am tired of him skirling 'Scotland for ever!' every time I meet him on the street. And I'm running out of excuses to keep from going to listen to him playing his bagpipes.

But I guess the biggest menace of all is Mrs. George Boddler. She is Mom's greatest friend. Mom can't do anything unless she consults Louise Boddler. They are always out and in each other's houses, though Mrs. Boddler is oftener in ours than in her own. She is a large shapeless dame, and she is always panting and out of breath. She and her little fat poodle, Bunny-Wunny, are a pair. If I'm not tripping over the one, I'm running full tilt into the other. It seems that Mrs. Boddler and Mom Winnegar have been great friends ever since they discovered they were both born on the 7th July. 'That was forty years ago,' Mom told me. 'Forty years since Louise came to stay in Struthers Bridge, and when she told me she'd been born on the seventh of July, too, right there and then we became buddies and we've been buddies ever since.'

Mom Winnegar is a great one for coincidences, but all I can say is it would take more than a coincidence like this to make me buddies with any of the other girls in Struthers Bridge. I reckon none of them like me much on account of Lew. They all thought they'd make him, so it was one in the eye for them when be brought back a bride from overseas. I can't say I blame them, because he's the nicest-looking fella in town.

Still, it's real wearing on me when one of them'll say sweet as you like: 'I always reckoned Lew was to be *my*

The Last G.I. Bride Wore Tartan

Mr. Right. He had quite a case on me, honey, before he went away to the War. Of course, I've got over him, *but . . .*'

When I hear things like that it makes me more determined to hang on to him. It's funny about me and Lew. When I grabbed him I was all set to be hard and calculating. I reckoned I was only marrying him so's I could get to Hollywood easy. But since I came to Struthers Bridge I'm not so sure about that. I've got kind of used to having Lew around. He's easy on the eye and he sure makes love in no uncertain fashion. I guess I'm getting kind of crazy about him.

This is what made me so mad when Isobel turned up unexpected a week ago.

X

I was on the porch mending a run in my stockings, listening to Pop Winnegar tell me all about the Struthers Bridge election campaign of 1911, when we saw the afternoon bus from St. Paul go past. 'Bus is on time to-day,' Pop said. 'Where's Mom? Reckon it's about time we had a cup of tea, ain't it, young woman? Gee, I must say I've sure got quick into your Scottish habits.'

Mom was in the lounge with Mrs. Boddler, so I shouted: 'Four-thirty, Mom! Pop's getting anxious about his tea!'

I bent over my stocking, trying not to hear Pop and hoping Mom wouldn't shout back she was too busy to make tea and would I make it. I was so busy pretending to be busy that I didn't notice anybody approaching the house until Bunny-Wunny began to yap and then I

The Last G.I. Bride Wore Tartan

heard Pop say: 'Here's a strange young woman luggin' some baggage!'

I looked up, and there was Isobel, smiling as bold as brass, and shoving Bunny-Wunny away with the edge of one of her suitcases.

'Darling!' she cried.

'Well, what do you know!' I said.

'How are you, dear?' she said, kissing me and looking at Pop as though she were all set to kiss him, too.

I introduced them quick, wondering what Isobel was doing here. I didn't like the look of those cases at all.

But in no time she'd told me it all. 'I couldn't stand Mervyn another minute, honey,' she said as soon as we were upstairs in my bedroom. 'Honest to goodness, ducky, what a poor fish he turned out to be. And what a joint that Rivers End is! My God, it's more like World's End. You never saw such a one-horse place, etc., etc.'

'So I've left him,' she said.

'Well, what do you know!' I said.

'I couldn't think where to go,' Isobel said. 'And as you were the nearest. . . . You don't mind putting me up, do you, honey, until I make up my mind what to do?'

'Well,' I said, but before I could explain about this not being my own house, and about Mom and Pop, she said: 'You're a pal, Scotty! I knew you wouldn't let me down. So if it's all right by you I'll just park myself here until I make up my mind whether I'm going straight back to Britain or whether I'll stay here until I get my divorce, etc., etc.'

'Now I must lash myself up to meet your folks,' she said, going to the mirror. 'Like Letty! Good old Letty, I wonder how she's getting on?'

'Fancy!' she cried, heaving on the lipstick. 'Mervyn

[43]

The Last G.I. Bride Wore Tartan

had the nerve to keep saying to me why didn't I try to look a bit more like Rita Hayworth. D'ya ever hear the like! I reckon he was pretty lucky to have somebody like me in a dump like Rivers End. Honest, ducky, you never saw such a dead-end hole. Rita Hayworth! . . . Huh, what's she got that I haven't got, etc., etc.? D'you know, kid, I've half a mind to stay here and try my luck on the movies. What say you and me hit the trail for Hollywood together?'

'Well,' I said.

'It would be nice to have a chum in a place like Hollywood,' Isobel said. 'At first, anyway, until we got properly going. We could live on our alimony.'

I was real thankful when Mom Winnegar shouted upstairs at that moment that tea was ready. I just didn't know what to make of Isobel, and I hustled her downstairs as quick as I could. 'Just a tick,' I said at the door of the lounge. 'I must collect my silk stockings from the porch before Bunny-Wunny gets a hold of them.'

'I never thought I'd find you mending the ladders in your stockings, Scotty,' Isobel said, following me on to the porch. 'I must say I thought Lew would of been able to keep you supplied with so many nylons from his store that you wouldn't of bothered about runs.'

'Nylons aren't so easy to get as all that,' I said.

'Well, for crying out loud,' Isobel said. 'Don't tell me Lew's a tight-wad! I must say I thought once or twice in New York——'

'Lew's all right,' I said. 'There's nothing wrong with Lew.'

'C'mon in and meet the folks,' I said opening the lounge door.

Isobel was hardly introduced to Mom and Mrs. Boddler before she'd launched into an account of how

The Last G.I. Bride Wore Tartan

she'd quarrelled with Mervyn and what she said to him and what he said to her. 'Of course, I should never have married him in the first place,' she said in her poshest tone. 'I should have made certain that he was able to keep me in the style to which I've been accustomed, etc. etc. It really is terribly hard on a girl like me when she discovers that the man she's given her all to is such an out-and-out blackguard. Why, there wasn't one thing that he'd told me true! He told me he was an executive in the oil business—and when I got there I found he worked a gasoline pump!'

'But I'm glad to see my little friend, Scotty, so happy and well settled,' she said, dabbing her eyes. 'I'm glad to see she's struck it lucky. She deserves it, because she had a hard time before she came over here, being a waitress, etc., etc.'

'Another cup of tea, Isobel?' I said.

'No, ducky; no thanks,' she said. 'But I'll have a cigarette, if I may.'

'But perhaps I shouldn't smoke,' she said, keeping her case half in and half out her bag. 'Perhaps your mother-in-law may object?'

'You don't mind, do you, Mrs. Winnegar?' she said, with a gushing smile. 'But of course you must be used to it by this time with Jessie smoking like a furnace!'

'Jessie doesn't smoke much,' Mom Winnegar said. 'Just two three a day is all Jessie smokes.'

'My, Scotty, you must have turned over a new leaf!' Isobel cried. 'A cigarette never seemed to be out of your mouth in the old days.'

'You and Jessie are old friends?' Mom said.

'Oh, yes, we've known each other for ages and ages,' Isobel said, leaning back and crossing her legs so that Pop Winnegar could get a good view.

The Last G.I. Bride Wore Tartan

'I must go now,' Mrs. Boddler said. 'George'll be home at any minute.'

She rose most unwillingly, keeping her eye on Isobel, hoping, I guess, she'd say some more before she finally went. But Isobel was smiling at Pop.

'I always like to be in when George comes home,' Louise Boddler said. 'I think a wife should always be there to greet her husband coming back from work.'

'Scotty's lucky in that respect, isn't she?' Isobel said. 'I'm sure she never needs to bother about being home to receive her husband when his mother's on the spot.'

'You *are* a lucky bag, Scotty!' she said. 'I bet you go gadding to the movies most afternoons, knowing that Mrs. Winnegar here will see to Lew's tea, etc., etc.'

'Jessie never goes to the movies without Lew,' Mom said.

'I really must go,' Mrs. Boddler said. 'Come along then, Bunny-Wunny. Home! Say good-bye to the ladies!'

'What a sweet little dog,' Isobel said. 'Isn't it, Scotty!'

'But of course, I forgot,' she said. 'I've just remembered that you loathe dogs.'

'I never——' I began, but just then Lew came in and Isobel rushed to him, crying: 'Lew! Lew love, how nice to see you!' And she kissed him before he knew where he was.

'I really must go now,' Mrs. Boddler said. 'I daren't put off another minute.'

And so she went, and I knew that before bedtime it would be all over Struthers Bridge about Isobel's arrival and what she'd said.

The Last G.I. Bride Wore Tartan

XI

'How long does that girl aim to stay here?' Mom Winnegar said on Isobel's third afternoon with us.

'Search me,' I said. 'I wish I knew.'

'She ain't doing herself any good staying here,' Mom said, sifting sugar into a basin with flour.

'Nor you,' she said, reaching for a packet of shredded suet.

'If I was her man I'd come and tan the pants offen her,' Mom went on, beginning to stir her cake mixture. 'She's no class. She's just no class at all. I can't think how you ever took up with her, Jessie.'

'I didn't take up with her at all,' I said. 'The shipping company put us both in the same cabin.'

'Well, all I can say is, it ain't right of the shipping company to do such things,' Mom said. 'She's no account and the quicker she gets on her way out of Struthers Bridge the better.'

But Isobel wasn't showing any signs of moving. She kept saying she was making her arrangements, but I couldn't see when she was doing them.

'Where is she now?' Mom Winnegar said.

'She said she was going to the post office,' I said.

'Well, girl, if I was you,' Mom Winnegar said, stirring quickly and not looking at me. 'If I was you,' she said, 'I'd go out and meet her. I reckon you should keep an eye on that young lady.'

'Okay,' I said, and as I walked slowly down the street towards the post office I thought maybe I'd misjudged Mom Winnegar a bit when I first came to Struthers Bridge. She wasn't a bad old stick. She had the size of that Isobel all right.

[47]

The Last G.I. Bride Wore Tartan

There was no sign of Isobel at the post office. Mamie Jones behind the counter said she'd been and gone an hour ago. I bought some stamps and began to walk back home. I was passing Pop's store, and I thought maybe I'd go in and see Lew, but as I was turning in the door who should come out but Isobel.

'Hello, ducks!' she cried, hitching her arm into mine. 'Out for a little constitutional? I must say I've enjoyed mine! I'm absolutely starving. Let's hurry back and get something to eat. I hope that mother-in-law of yours has the tea ready.'

'I was goin' in to see Lew,' I said.

'He's terrible busy, etc., etc.,' Isobel said. 'He just about flung me out on my neck. Don't bother him just now, ducks. Come on!'

She began to draw me up the street, so I went, not wanting to make any fuss. I'd seen old Mr. Neill heading for the store anyway.

'Hello, how's my little Scottish friend to-day?' he shouted, waving his stick.

'Fine, thank you,' I called, and I waved, but I didn't make any move to stop.

'Who's that old geezer, honey?' Isobel said. 'God, I must say there are a lot of queer guys in this dump. You've certainly landed amongst them, etc., etc. The quicker you get out of it and away from them the better.'

'Och, it's not a bad place,' I said. 'And old Mr. Neill isn't a bad old soul.'

'Don't make me laugh,' Isobel said. 'What about packing up and lighting out with me to-morrow for Hollywood?'

'So you're going to-morrow?' I said.

'Well, I haven't made up my mind definitely yet,'

The Last G.I. Bride Wore Tartan

she said. 'I've been trying to figure out how much money I've got. Can you raise any?'

'No, I guess not,' I said.

'What about the Winnegars?' she said. 'Would they loan me some?'

'Well, really, Isobel!' I said, feeling I'd just about had enough.

'All right, if you don't want to help me,' she said, 'I guess I'll get along all right with what I've got. But I just thought because we were pals, etc., etc.

'If you're as dependent on the Winnegars as all that,' she said.

'But I'm sorry for you, Scotty,' she said. 'With that old battle-axe of a mother-in-law. I bet you'll be glad when you get your divorce.'

'Who said anything about a divorce?' I said. 'You needn't think because you and Mervyn can't hit it off that everybody's like you.'

'And there's nothing wrong with my mother-on-law,' I said. 'She's been very nice to me.'

So Isobel shut up then, and after we'd had tea she went away and wrote letters.

XII

I'd thought Lew had been kind of funny ever since Isobel came, but I'd put it down to him not liking her very much and to her landing on his folks in this way. Still, that evening he hardly spoke, and he went away to bed early. Normally when he went to bed early he'd say no matter who was there: 'C'mon, honey, beddybyes!' and he'd practically push me away in front of him. But that night he just picked up a magazine and said: 'Well, I'm hittin' the hay.'

The Last G.I. Bride Wore Tartan

He was lying with his back to me when I went into our room, and he never spoke or turned round while I undressed. 'Are you asleep already?' I said, but he never answered.

I got in beside him and I put my arm round him, but he shoved my hand away with his elbow and said: 'Aw, lay off me, can't you! I've had a heavy day and I'm tired.'

I lay and looked at his broad shoulders for a few minutes, then I put my arm round him again.

'Darling,' I said.

'Aw for Chrissake!' he said. 'I was near asleep.'

'What's the matter, honey?' I said.

He shoved my arm away again.

'Can't you leave a fella in peace?' he said. 'Move over to your own side of the bed.'

'But, darling,' I said.

'Aw, go to sleep,' he said.

I lay for two three minutes, then I started to cry.

'Aw shuttup,' Lew said. 'If you don't quit it I'll go to the spare room.'

I cried all the louder at this.

'What's the matter?' I said. 'What've I done?'

'What've you not done!' Lew said.

'That Isobel,' he said.

'Yeah, that Isobel,' he said again. 'Pal of yours. Just the right kinda pal for a dame like you. She came into the store to-day and did she open her mouth and spill it!'

'Yeah, did she spill it!' he said, heaving round on to his back.

'So you thought you'd play me for a sucker, did you?' he said.

'And how soon do you plan to file suit for divorce, Mrs. Winnegar?' he said.

I was weeping buckets by this time. If that Isobel had

[50]

The Last G.I. Bride Wore Tartan

been within reach I don't know what I'd have done to her.

'I'm not,' I said, 'I'm not aiming to file for divorce.'

'Since when?' Lew said. 'Isobel told me you had your mind made up to file for divorce before you left England.'

'I had not,' I said.

'You had so,' he said. 'Isobel told me.'

'Isobel's a liar,' I said.

'Isn't that just like a dame!' he said. 'She can't even stick to her pals.'

'You just married me so's you could get to the States,' he said. 'Everybody on the boat knew it.'

'I did not,' I said.

'I love you,' I said.

'Tell that to all the other guys,' he said. 'You're just practising so's you'll have it word-perfect when you get to Hollywood.'

'I'm never going to Hollywood,' I said.

'Don't let me stop you,' he said. 'I wouldn't want to ruin your career.'

'I don't want a career,' I said. 'Not any more I don't.'

'I just want you,' I said.

'Well, think again,' Lew said.

And he got up and went to the spare room and locked the door. I was going to beat on the door until he opened it, but it was right next to Isobel's room, so I didn't. I went back to bed and wept and wept until I fell asleep.

XIII

The next morning when I got up Lew had left for the store. Mom Winnegar was in the kitchen and she just gave me one look and then she said: 'If I was you,

The Last G.I. Bride Wore Tartan

girl, I'd do somethin' about those eyes of yours before that Isobel gets up. I reckon your pillows must be sopping.'

'And I wouldn't worry if I were you!' she shouted after me. 'That Isobel's gonna get a spoke in her wheel or my name ain't Gert Winnegar.'

I didn't think much about this at the time, I was too busy figuring how I was going to put a spoke in Isobel's wheel on my own. But I remembered it later when Mervyn arrived.

Isobel was having her breakfast and I was giving her a good piece of my mind when Mom Winnegar came in and said: 'Guy here to see you, Isobel.'

And there right behind Mom was a tall fella that I recognised at once from his pictures.

'Mervyn!' Isobel yelled.

'What're you doin' here?' she said.

'I've come to take you home,' he said. 'There ain't never been a divorce in our family.'

'There ain't never been a divorce in our family either,' Mom Winnegar chipped in. 'And there ain't gonna be one if I can help it. You'd better find out here and now that America ain't just what they make it out to be in the movies. Folks like us don't go in for divorce as much as they make out.'

'How d'ya know I was here?' Isobel said.

'A little bird whispered,' Mervyn said.

'A pretty big bird I should think,' Isobel said, looking at Mom Winnegar.

'Yeah, I phoned him yesterday when you were down at the store making mischief,' Mom said. 'But I guess it's the last mischief you're gonna make here.'

'You bet,' Mervyn said. 'Better get your stuff together, honey. We're leavin' on the next bus.'

The Last G.I. Bride Wore Tartan

'We are not,' Isobel said.

She got into a right paddy then and yelled and yelled. But it was no good. Mervyn and Mom were as firm as a couple of Rocks of Gibraltar. 'You get her on that bus, young man,' Mom said to Mervyn. 'Then you can thrash things out for yourselves.'

'Though it's her I'd thrash,' she said. 'Soundly.'

'I'm right sorry for that boy marryin' a tramp like that,' she said when they'd gone. 'I reckon she won't go a step further than St. Paul.'

'Still, it'll be the best thing for him if she don't,' she said.

'Now you go and get your face fixed,' she said to me. 'Then go down to the store and tell that husband of yours he's a sap to listen to anythin' a tramp like that'd tell him.'

XIV

Lew wasn't at the store. One of the girls said he'd got in the flivver and left soon after they opened. 'Looked kinda funny, Lew did,' she said. 'Kinda peaky.'

'He didn't sleep well last night,' I said. 'His stomach was bothering him.'

Louise Boddler was in when I got home, and she and Mom were having a right good session in the kitchen, so I went up to my room.

I was in a real panic. I thought about all the things that had happened last night and I sat down in front of the dressing-table and wept and wept. I could have strangled that Isobel. I was so mad at her. What right had she to come here and make trouble between me and

The Last G.I. Bride Wore Tartan

Lew? I just hoped Mervyn would give her a good hiding. Though I reckoned Mom was right and Isobel wouldn't go a step further than St. Paul. I bet she'd take the first boat back to England, like so many other G.I. Brides. And that was the right place for her, I reckoned. Good riddance to bad rubbish and all that. The lousy tramp. It was real bad luck that I'd been put in the same cabin as no-class dames like her and Cora and Letty. I bet they'd lit out by this time, too, and were on the middle of the Atlantic. Pity the boat wouldn't sink and drown them all.

I got so het up thinking about them that I stopped crying. I sat and looked at myself in the glass. You'd have thought with all the crying I'd done in the past twenty-four hours that I'd have looked a sight. But I didn't look any too bad. In fact I looked all right. I looked pretty good. As good as Ginger Rogers or Bette Davis when they were having a big weepy scene.

Better than them, I thought, giving myself the once-over. The way the tears were hanging on my lashes was real artistic. I bet if a director saw me like this he'd sign me up and put me on the first train for Hollywood.

Of course, Hollywood was out of the question now. I'd been daft ever to think of such a thing. I wasn't thinking about anything else now but Lew. I was for Lew in a big way. I just didn't want anything but him, and for him to put his arms tight around me.

I went down and helped Mom prepare the lunch. Mrs. Boddler hurried away after her session with Mom, so excited she could hardly take time to say hello to me.

We laid the lunch, but though Pop came in Lew never appeared. We waited a while, then we had ours. Mom put aside Lew's to keep hot for him, saying: 'I'll make his ears hot for him when he comes.'

The Last G.I. Bride Wore Tartan

But three o'clock came and he never turned up. Then four o'clock. I began to get in a real stew, wondering what had happened to him, and I had all sorts of visions of the flivver having gone over a cliff with Lew lying at the bottom among the wreckage. . . .

XV

It was six o'clock before Lew turned up. Mom and Pop had gone out visiting, and I was walking up and down, up and down. Because by this time I was near demented.

'Where've you been?' I cried.

'What does it matter to you where I've been?' he said.

'It matters a lot,' I said. 'Keepin' folk worryin' about you.'

'Fat lot of worryin' you'll do,' he said.

'Bring on the eats,' he said. 'I'm starvin'.'

'Bring on the eats!' I cried. 'Here am I near demented and all you think about is your stomach.'

'Well, I couldn't sleep last night on account of my stomach,' he said. 'So Kitty in the store told me.'

'It was news to me, I must say,' he said, parking himself at the table.'

'Well, it'll be news to you, too, that Isobel has gone,' I said, putting his hotted-up lunch in front of him. 'Mervyn came and took her away.'

'Whyn't he take you, too?' Lew said, beginning to wolf. 'Or are you waitin' for this Paul Whatsisname to come and cart you off?'

'What Paul Whatsisname?' I said.

'You know,' he said. 'Fella you fell for on the boat.'

'I didn't fall for any fella on the boat,' I said. 'I only fell for you.'

The Last G.I. Bride Wore Tartan

'Don't try to come the bag,' Lew said. 'Isobel told me about this Paul guy.'

'Isobel's a liar,' I said.

'So you told me last night,' he said. 'I still don't believe it.'

I started to weep then. It was about time. 'You'd believe Isobel before you'd believe me,' I said.

'Why shouldn't I?' he said.

'But I'm your wife,' I said.

'Thought you were gonna sue for divorce,' he said.

'Oh, Lew!' I cried.

'You know I wouldn't,' I said.

'Paul meant nothin' to me,' I said. 'He was just a guy I danced with on the boat.'

'Isobel said she saw you kissin' him,' Lew said.

'What if I did?' I said. 'It was just once. I couldn't help it. I was thinkin' about you at the time, and he reminded me of you. Honest he did.'

'So I'm to spend my life watchin' out for fellas that remind you of me,' Lew said, getting up and switching on the radio.

'You know you aren't!' I shouted, to make myself heard above a dame crooning *Give Me Five Minutes More*.

'Looks like it,' he said, sitting down and opening a magazine.

'Listen, honey,' I said.

'You know I'm for you in a big way,' I said, wiping my eyes. 'Ever since that night in the taxi.'

'That taxi,' he said.

'Why won't you believe me?' I said, weeping harder than ever.

'Aw, cut it out,' he said. 'Let's call it a day.'

I don't know what I said next, but in between crying I tried to tell him all about Birnieburn and wanting to

[56]

The Last G.I. Bride Wore Tartan

go to Hollywood and how I didn't want to go there any longer and how I'd never been and never would be in love with anybody but him. And then quite suddenly he put his arms round me and said: 'Aw, honey, let's forget it. . . .

'Stop cryin', sweetheart,' he said after a while. 'You're gonna make your eyes all red, and I wouldn't like that.'

'I can't,' I said, 'I can't.'

And I couldn't, because the harder I tried to stop the harder I cried. I laid my head against Lew's shoulder and he took my hankie and wiped the tears as fast as they fell. We stood like that for a long time, and then I said: 'Let me go, love. I must go and fix my face before Mom and Pop come back.'

But Lew held on to me tight, humming: 'Give me five minutes more, only five minutes more, let me stay, let me stay in your arms. . . .'

'Ach, you'll get plenty of time for that yet,' I said. 'Lemme go.'

'Aw, what's the hurry,' he said.

'Do you remember that last night in London?' he said.

'Will I ever forget it,' I said.

'That's the way I feel now,' he said. 'That's the way I'll always feel about you, baby,' he said.

'Me too,' I said.

'Now I really must go and fix my face,' I said, and I kissed him and ran upstairs.

And while I was lashing myself up, so that I'd be all right for Mom and Pop coming home, I noticed the *G.I. Bride's Guide* lying on my dressing-table, and I thought of all the things it didn't tell you. And I thought as I ran downstairs to Lew, that maybe one day I'd try and write a better one myself—if I could get time to get round to doing it between films.

HUNT THE SLIPPER

SALLY took her place in the queue at ten o'clock. She had seen the sandals the evening before, and she was determined to get them. They were the exact blue of her new dress, and the bright scarlet straps would go perfectly with it. She would buy a scarlet scarf . . . or maybe a little scarlet waistcoat would be better? She tried to make up her mind as she watched the women in front of her.

The girl with the high black hat was telling the woman next her that she'd been there since twenty-five-past nine. 'It's cruel, isn't it, ducks, to have to wait all this time for a pair of shoes?' she said.

'Yes, and when you get in they tell you they haven't got your size!' the other woman said.

'Oh, for the good old days before the War!' the girl with the black hat sighed.

'Well, I dunno,' the other woman said. 'I guess I'd kinda miss the queues if they was done away with, wouldn't you, love?'

'That's right,' Black Hat said. 'They're nice and matey.'

Sally sighed with exasperation. She turned up her eyes, and wheeled round to look in the window. The sandals were still there in the corner. Pray God nobody snaffled them before her turn came.

Ten-past ten. She began to get agitated. She'd told Terry to meet her here at ten o'clock and to bring the money with him. It wasn't like him to be late.

Hunt the Slipper

Still, ten minutes was nothing these days in London. No matter how well you thought you judged it, you couldn't always reckon with Tubes and traffic blocks. Terry would turn up all right. He always did.

But what if he didn't? What if she got into the shop, got her shoes and was handed the bill? What was she to say then?

She began to rehearse. 'My friend's coming with the money. I gave him a cheque and he was to go to the bank to cash it. I don't know what's happened to him. . . .'

No, that wouldn't do. Better say: 'My husband's coming with the money.' Only . . . Terry didn't look like anybody's husband. Terry was all right, but Terry had that rakish bachelor look about him. Heavens, it would be such a take-down if she got the length of getting the sandals and then had to go into a lot of detail about paying for them. She was a fool; she should have made certain yesterday that she had enough money. But of course, she had seen the sandals only last night after the banks were closed.

'I met ever such a nice girl in a queue last week,' the girl in the black hat was saying. 'An actress she was. In the chorus of that show at the Rialto. Oooo, she was ever so nice. And ever so lady-like. Not like a chorus girl at all.'

'You can't tell these days, can you, ducks?' the woman next her said. 'Nobody ever is what they seem to be.'

That was right, Sally thought. Now, nobody would ever take her for a respectable farmer's wife from Aberdeenshire on holiday in the Big City. Or would they? Did she look like a country cousin?

No, she didn't! No country cousin would ever dare to buy those blue and scarlet sandals. Stout sensible

Hunt the Slipper

brogues, that was what everybody expected the country cousin to buy.... And maybe that was what her mother-in-law and Bill would expect her to buy. She could just hear them and see the looks on their faces. 'Oh, Sally! Whatever made you buy those silly things for, dear? They're not *suitable*.'

Suitable.... She was tired of having things that were suitable and sensible. She wanted something frivolous and gay for a change. And those sandals were the thing!

She took another look. They were still in the window. The queue was beginning to move a little. Dear God, if one of those other women had her eye on them she would pass out. She would go absolutely paralytic with horror.

Paralytic.... She giggled to herself and changed it into a cough. Paralytic.... That was one of the words Maisie was always using. Life was paralytic. Parties were paralytic. People were paralytic. Just wait until she went home and said to Bill: 'Don't expect me to visit those paralytic people, the Meldrums, again!'

What was keeping Terry? It was twenty-past ten. My God, what could have happened to him? It wasn't like him to be late. Whatever Terry's faults he was always punctual. Even Maisie, who hated Terry's guts and said he was the most paralytically perverse person she'd ever met, had to admit that he was always on time.

Twenty-five-past ten and here she was almost at the door. She began to rehearse in agitation. 'My husband is coming with the money.' 'My friend is coming with the money.' God, it was like learning French. *Mon mari ou mon ami*! She could just imagine the look the assistant would give her if she said 'my husband' and then Terry

Hunt the Slipper

turned up. But would that be worse than the kind of look she would get if she said 'my friend?' Whichever way you looked at it the prospect didn't look any too bright.

There was a sudden spurt of movement. For a moment, as she approached the door, Sally wondered whether she should hang back and allow some of the people behind her to go first. But if she did, that might mean losing the sandals. She tried to make up her mind quickly, and she was just opening her mouth to say 'I think I'll wait,' when the man at the door put up his hand and said: 'No more, madam.'

She was first in the queue! She sagged against the corner of the door. If this was a movie this would be the moment for Terry to appear, triumphantly waving a bunch of bank-notes. But it wasn't a movie, so she began to rehearse again. She simply mustn't lose these sandals. They were still there.

'You're a fine one!'

Sally jumped at the accusing tone. This wasn't the answer she expected from any shop assistant to her carefully worded story of the money that had never come. It took her a second to adjust herself.

'Hello, Terry!' she grinned. 'Where have you been!'

'Where have I not been!' He leaned wearily against the door beside her, pushing in between her and the woman behind. Sally just had time to notice this as she prepared to listen to his explanation. Terry was always rude to women—far ruder to them than some other women could be. That was part of his charm.

'I thought you said the Cumfy Shoe Shop was at the Marble Arch end of Oxford Street?' he said.

'Well, so it is.'

'You women!' He blew cigarette smoke angrily into

[61]

Hunt the Slipper

the air. 'This isn't the Marble Arch end, ducky, this is the Tottenham Court Road end.'

'Is it!' Sally opened her eyes wide. 'Isn't that rare! What a fine chase you must have had!'

'Did you get the money?' she said.

'Give me time to get my breath,' Terry said.

He took out his wallet and handed her twenty-five pounds.

'Oh, what rare!' Sally said. 'What a fine time I'm going to have with this!'

'You're fairly getting through the cash, ducky,' Terry said.

'Well, why not?' She laughed. 'It's not often the country cousin comes to town. Bill'll throw a fit when I go home and say how much I've spent.'

'You and Maisie between you!' Terry said. 'How is my dear friend Maisie?'

'She's all right,' Sally said.

'Did she send me her love?'

'I couldn't look you truthfully in the eye and say that.' Sally laughed. 'She asked what I was going to see "that paralytically perverse creature" for; and so I said I was forced to see you because you were the only person I knew in London with a bank account who would change a cheque for me.'

'Dear Maisie,' Terry said.

He opened his case and looked at his last cigarette. 'Are you going to be long in here?'

Sally shrugged. 'It depends. The last batch of people who went in are still there. But there's no reason why you should wait for me,' she said. 'I know you're a busy little bee, so run along and get about your business.'

'I'm doing nothing this morning,' Terry said. 'I thought I'd help you spend that twenty-five quid—

Hunt the Slipper

before friend Maisie gets her claws on it—and what's left of it after you come out of this place! Anyway, I'd rather like to see inside this superb mausoleum. I might get off with one of the assistants.'

'I'll tag along with you, if you don't mind,' he said.

'I don't mind at all,' Sally said. 'If you can be bothered waiting I'll stand you a cup of coffee after I've bought my sandals.'

'Coffee?' Terry raised an eyebrow. 'Nothing else?'

'Coffee,' Sally said.

'I think I'll dash away and see if I can get some cigarettes,' he said. 'If you get in before I get back, I'll come in and collect you.'

Terry had been gone about three minutes when the man at the door said: 'This way, madam.'

He put Sally in the charge of a madonna-like creature, swathed in black silk, who swept ahead of her, saying: 'Come this way, please.'

Sally followed her up one side of a curved chromium-plated staircase set in the middle of the shop. Goodness, she thought, as her feet sank into the rich pile of the carpet, there's nothing so swanky as this in Aberdeen. Just wait until I get home and tell them what a palace of a place it is!

'Take those seats along there, please,' the floor-walker said, waving a slim white hand from the women who were following Sally to a row of empty green leather chairs with chromium arms and legs.

Sally went to the furthest chair and seated herself gingerly. It was easy seen that this shop didn't cater for rather hefty young farmers' wives from the country. Mercy on us, she thought, as she felt the chair slipping forward on the carpet, what'll happen if I do a nose-dive!

Hunt the Slipper

But all was well. She settled herself comfortably and looked about. Rows and rows of chairs were filled by all sorts of women, waiting patiently. Some yawned; some stared moodily at the carpet; one across the floor from Sally was knitting energetically. Here and there one was trying on a pair of shoes. A few bored-looking assistants glided about with a shoe in their hands.

Sally lit a cigarette and looked about for a place to put the burnt match. She could see no ash-trays. She was just wondering whether she should grind it into the thick carpet—seeing a headline: FARMER'S WIFE BURNS DOWN WEST END SHOP—when the woman next her said: 'That's the ash-tray there.'

'Mercy on us!' Sally said. 'So it is!'

She pulled the tall cuspidor-like article towards her. 'It's real bonnie, isn't it?' she said. 'I thought it was a vase for flowers!'

The woman smiled, then she looked at the carpet, showing no inclination to enter into conversation. Maybe she doesn't understand my Aberdeen accent, thought Sally, though I thought I'd spoken in real good Oxford English!

'Yes?'

A tall, pale girl with peroxided hair was standing before her, looking over her head in a disdainful manner.

'Oh, is it my turn?' Sally looked up brightly. 'You've an awful bonnie pair of sandals in your window. Blue with red straps. I'd like to try them on.'

'What size?'

'Sevens,' Sally said.

'I'm afraid they'd be too small for you,' the girl said, brushing away the curls from her little pink ears.

'They look like my size,' Sally said.

'No, I'm afraid they're too small,' the girl said. She

Hunt the Slipper

stood with one hand on her hip, looking down at the toe of her smart black suede shoe tapping the carpet.

'Let me try them on, anyway,' Sally said.

'I'm sure they're too small, madam,' the girl said.

Sally leaned forward, smiling coaxingly. 'Just let me have a wee shottie of them,' she said. 'Maybe I could manage to squeeze into them.'

'They're near the front of the window, aren't they?' the girl said. 'I'm afraid I can't get them out, madam, if they aren't likely to fit you.'

'I whiles take six-and-a-halves,' Sally said. 'I can even squeeze into sixes if necessary.'

She leaned back and looked grimly at the girl.

Peroxided hair sighed and looked up at the chromium and glass ceiling. 'I warn you, madam,' she said. 'It's quite hopeless for you to try them. Quite hopeless. They're for a small foot.'

'Let me try, anyway,' Sally said.

The girl shrugged and drifted away majestically. Sally looked at the woman next her and said: 'Might as well give her something to do to earn her salary!'

'That's right,' the woman said. 'You'd think some of those girls were doing you a favour the way they carry on. Saucy pieces!'

Sally lit another cigarette. A girl with auburn hair came and said 'Are you being attended to?' to the woman next her.

'Have you anything in fawn with wedged heels?' the woman said.

'Sorry,' the girl with auburn hair said, and she looked at her nails.

'Anything else in fawn?' the woman said. 'A pair of court suedes maybe?'

'Nothing,' the girl said.

Hunt the Slipper

The woman rose and looked at Sally. They smiled at each other, then with a slight shrug the woman left the shop.

Sally saw the peroxided blonde moving slowly up the stair-case, dangling a blue and red sandal.

She held it out disdainfully. 'I'm sure you'll find it too small.'

Sally took off her well-worn sensible brown brogue. 'Mercy on us!' she said. 'I didn't know I had a hole in my stocking! I should have attended to that before I came here, shouldn't I!'

But peroxided hair did not even smile. She stood staring at the well of the staircase in a bored fashion.

'Have you a shoe-horn?' Sally said.

Peroxided hair moved slowly to a small table and, picking up a long horn, she held it out without speaking.

Sally grinned as she bent to try on the sandal. What a time she would have imitating this assistant's airs and graces to Bill!

She sat back triumphantly. 'It fits!'

The assistant raised her eyebrows in an unbelieving manner. 'Really? You look as though you have a much bigger foot than that.'

'It fits perfectly,' Sally said. 'I'll just stand up and try it.'

She took a few experimental steps. 'Lovely,' she said. 'I'll try on the other one now.'

'All right.' The assistant moved slowly towards the staircase. Sally watched her, smiling at the queenly way the girl trailed her hand down the chromium railing.

She was looking at her feet in a mirror when Terry bounded up the stair and came towards her. 'Being served?'

'Ay, isn't it bonnie?' She held out her foot.

Hunt the Slipper

'Very nice.' He grinned. 'But what will Bill say when he sees them? They're hardly the kind of thing for cleaning out cow-sheds, are they?'

'I never set foot in the cow-byres,' Sally said. 'I have three maids!'

The assistant glanced at Terry when she returned with the other sandal. 'They look very nice, madam,' she said when Sally had both of them on. 'Aren't they?' she said, and she smiled at Terry.

Sally smiled down at the sandals. They were very pretty and they fitted perfectly. She looked up quickly as she heard the assistant say to Terry:

'It's difficult to suit people these days when both stock and assistants are scarce—especially people like your friend who need something individual.'

Sally looked again at the sandals. They were awful bonnie, and they fitted fine. And she had plenty of money and coupons . . . and she'd stood all that time in the queue. . . .

'Ay, we'll keep these by us in the meantime,' she said, in her broadest Aberdeenshire accent. 'Now, I wonder if you'd let me see a pair of black suedes—rather like those you've got on yourself, only with not such high silly heels.'

'Certainly, madam.' The assistant smiled brightly at Terry and glided away. Sally noticed that she walked much more quickly than she'd been doing, and she was swaying slightly at the hips. She looked at Terry and grinned. Terry grinned back, stroking his small black moustache.

'You must have something that takes,' Sally said.

'Poisonality plus!' He laughed.

'Well, you'd better use it on that dame,' Sally said. 'She needs a change of heart!'

Hunt the Slipper

While Sally tried on a smart black court suede, the peroxide blonde flirted outrageously with Terry. She had become animated quite suddenly. Sally alternately frowned and smiled from one shoe to the other. Really she had set her heart on those sandals. They were awful bonnie, and she had the coupons and she had plenty of money. And despite what Terry said, she knew that Bill would like them. Bill liked her to wear nice things. In fact, he would probably want her to take both pairs. There was really no reason why she shouldn't. But . . .

She looked from Terry to the assistant and frowned.

She put on her own shoe slowly, looking at the sandals. Then she rose, tucking her bag under her arm. 'No, I doubt none of these will suit me,' she said, smiling sweetly at the assistant. 'They're just too individual. Far too fancy for a simple country cousin like me. I think I'll wait until I get back to Aberdeen and buy something stout and sensible to suit my personality.'

'Good morning,' she said, taking Terry's arm.

'Come along, dear,' she said to him. 'I'll stand you a coffee.'

I MARRIED THREE ACTRESSES

I was tickling the ivories in a dump in Denver when I met my first wife. Natasha was a crooner. She joined our three-piece band one day, and I married her a week later. It was a neck-to-neck race between me and the drummer. I must say Gus was pretty good about it. 'You got in your Big Note first, buddy,' he said.

For three months we were crazily happy. We were a small-time band in a small-time dump, but we were going places. Natasha and me had a nice little apartment, and every two or three nights we had friends in and made whoopee. Natasha was the cutest babe, with slinky black hair and almond-shaped eyes. Her old man had been a White Russian general, she said, but her mother was a true dyed-in-the-wool American. She was raised in a small town in the Middle West and as far as she was concerned Denver was the Big City. But she didn't aim to stay there. No, sir! Natasha had her eye on the lights of old Broadway. 'We ain't gonna stick here all our lives, Hank,' she kept telling me. 'We're young. We're gonna be stars yet.'

'I'm with you, baby,' I said. 'A hundred per cent.'

We got our chance when Bindy Norton came to town. Bindy was on the look-out for a band for his new place in Forty-second Street. A week later we'd hit New York. I reckon it was Natasha's singing that did it. Her singing and the way she looked at Bindy out of those narrow eyes.

Not that I ever thought Natasha wasn't on the level.

I Married Three Actresses

'I'm crazy about you, big boy,' she told me, and I believed her.

We were a sure-fire hit at Bindy's place, and it wasn't long before he graded us up to one of his places on Broadway itself. We'd hit the jack-pot all right.

NATASHA AND THE THREE NIMBLE-WITS. Gee, it was good to see our name in lights. I often used to stand across the street and look at it before going in for our session. Me and Andy got a big kick out of it. I guess we got more kick out of it than either Natasha or Gus. But then Andy was just a hick from Ohio, and I started in a small town myself.

'Aw, why waste your time staring at 'em,' Natasha used to say. 'You ain't seen nothin' yet. We're goin' bigger places than this.'

'This is just chicken-feed,' she said.

I believed her. There was something about Natasha that made you believe she'd do what she said. Look at the way she took the stand at the trial. She was front-page news all right. I knew I'd hitched my wagon to a star.

But what I didn't know was that the star wasn't keen about having any followers. I didn't realise it for a long time. I thought me and Natasha were still quite happy with each other. We'd a larger apartment now and we had more friends in for drinks, but things were still the way they'd always been with us.

Maybe we had too many friends in for drinks. I didn't notice it at the time. It was Andy who pointed it out to me. Andy might be a hick, but there was a lot of grey matter parked somewhere inside his fair curly head.

'Natasha's two-timin' you,' he said.

I was all set to take a poke at him, but he was bigger and stronger than me. 'Take it easy, Hank,' he said,

I Married Three Actresses

holding my wrists. 'I ain't tellin' you this because I want to. I been holdin' out on you for weeks, but I reckon I had to tell you some time.'

'Who is it?' I said. 'Gus?'

'No, Gus isn't in on this,' Andy said. 'Though maybe you might as well know that Gus was in the running when we were still in Denver. Gus and a few other guys.'

'It's Wally Coulter,' he said.

Wally Coulter was what used to be called a Big Shot gangster, only they don't call them gangsters any more. Wally was horning in on the night-club cabaret racket. He was in a fair way to being Bindy Norton's only rival. He'd been hanging around us for a while, and he'd been up at the apartment for drinks, but I hadn't thought much of it.

I tackled Natasha at once. Bull-headed, that's me. When I've got something to say or do I go right ahead with it. No velvet-gloved methods for this kiddo.

'Well, if you must know,' Natasha said, 'it's true.'

She was wearing a black velvet gown that slinked all over her. You could see every muscle when she moved. She leaned against the dressing table, filing her nails.

'Wally's gonna star me in a new club he's openin',' she said, pitching her cigarette butt into the empty grate. 'He's gonna star me—*alone*.'

'What about me and the boys?' I said.

'You'd better take the first train back to the Dust Bowl, brother,' she said. 'You've seen the writing on the wall.'

Maybe I had. But I'd seen something else, too. I took a couple of good pokes at Natasha and walked out. Her lawyer said the black eye I gave her was sufficient grounds, and she got the divorce all right.

And so me and the boys were out on our necks.

I Married Three Actresses

Bindy was having no more of us. I said we'd get another crooner to take Natasha's place, but Bindy said no dice. 'I only signed you on account of that dame,' he said. 'Sorry, boys, but it's good-bye.'

And so the Three Nimble-Wits had to get out in the sticks again. We got another crooner, a blonde baby this time, name of Bertha. And this time it was Gus who made her. I was off dames, I told him, he could go right ahead.

Sometimes I thought when I remembered how Gus had two-timed me with Natasha in Denver that I might do the same with him. Bertha gave me lots of encouragement. She was a nice baby all right, but she was too like Natasha for my taste. Men, men, and yet more men, that was all these two dames thought about.

My second wife, Minnie Valence, was different. All that Minnie was interested in was drink. That guy in *The Lost Week End* had nothing on her.

Minnie was a Burlesque Queen in the small-time circuits. She was big and buxom, with vivid red hair, and when she came on dressed in tights and pranced up and down singing Sophie Tucker kind of songs the hicks in those two-cent places fell for her in a big way.

Everything was big about Minnie. She was bighearted, big-mouthed, and a big boozer. She was so big she swamped you. She near swamped me completely the three months I was married to her.

I only took up with Minnie to escape Bertha. At that time we were doing a vaudeville circuit, being billed as *Bertha and the Three Bumble-Wits*. It was the same set-up as we'd had with Natasha except that me and Gus had switched places. And in the same way as Natasha two-timed me, Bertha was two-timing Gus. I didn't feel sorry for Gus. He had it coming.

But I was having no dealings with Bertha. That babe

I Married Three Actresses

wasn't in my line. Maybe Minnie wasn't either. But I reckoned I'd rather collide with a ten-ton truck than a man-eating monoplane.

Me and Minnie had a slap-up wedding. A proper theatrical do, with champagne flying. Bertha was mistress of ceremonies, reception hostess or what have you. Dressed in a leopard-skin coat and a cute little hat made of green feathers, she was the life and soul of the party. I kept looking at her every now and then, expecting her to crack a whip as she rounded up the guests and made them do their tricks. Bertha sure ought to have been ring-mistress in a circus. Either that or behind the bars. Few man-eating tigers had anything on her.

'Here's happy days, Hank!' she toasted me.

'Thanks a lot,' I said.

I felt I'd need all the good luck I could get. I'd had an eyeful of Minnie pushing back the drinks and already I was scared. She was pretty well plastered.

She kept plastered all the three months we were together. I often wondered how she managed to go on and do her numbers. But she was remarkable. I guess none of the hicks she held in the palm of her hand ever thought she was tight as she waggled her big bottom at them and hollered: 'You've gotta love a little, kiss a little, that's the stooory of love!'

This is the story of love all right. Sometimes I used to see those hicks look at me with envy as me and Minnie came out of the stage door. I reckon they were remembering the words of the song she sometimes sang: 'Howdya like to spoon with me? Dangle me upon your knee?' Thinking me and Minnie were going home to do that.

Yeah, imagine me with nearly sixteen stone of solid flesh on my lap. A skinny little runt like me! Don't make

I Married Three Actresses

me laugh, brother. For it was no laughing matter hoisting Minnie into bed when she was so tight she couldn't stand straight. And it was no laughing matter either sitting with her through the night, holding her hand when she got the D.T.s.

I can't remember how Kate came into my life. I reckon I must have met her two-three times before she ever registered. She was a friend of Minnie's.

I guess she was a strange friend for Minnie to have. She was legit. and she had all the high-hattedness of the legit. for poor vaudevillians like me and Minnie. But I guess it isn't so strange now that I look back and realise just what Kate's racket was. Minnie was a big, fine buxom dame, and she sure had sex-appeal.

It was Kate who told me Minnie wasn't going to last long. We were playing in Cincinnati at the time. Minnie and our three-piece were on the same bill at one of the vaudeville theatres down-town, but Kate was at one of the main theatres. She was starring in a try-out that was heading for Broadway. Her name was on all the bill-boards. KATHERINE JASSY. PERSONAL APPEARANCE OF THE GREAT BROADWAY STAR. And she was staying at the principal hotel, while us poor goofs were at a third-rate boarding-house. Kate was in the money all right.

She looked classy, too. She went in for a line in smart tailor-mades and wore practically no jewellery. And what she did wear was good. It had Cartier stamped on every link. She made dames like Bertha look like flophouse floosies.

Bertha didn't like Kate. And Kate didn't like Bertha. Which was funny, I reckon, because whatever else Bertha was she sure had loads of sex-appeal.

Me and Gus and Bertha were lunching one day in a

I Married Three Actresses

restaurant down town. We were expecting Minnie to join us. She'd had a date at the hairdresser's and I was beginning to figure she was late, when Kate walked in and sat down at our table. We weren't the only ones who stared. Everybody in the place twisted their necks to have a better look, and you could hear the whisper going round: 'That's Katherine Jassy.'

I could see that Bertha didn't know how to take it. She hated Kate's guts. But she liked the attention our table was causing, and she preened herself, even though it was only reflected glory.

'Where's Minnie?' I said.

'Minnie's in hospital.' Kate took off her gloves and laid them on the table. 'She's in a bad way, Hank. You'd better go along there at once.'

Bertha perked up at this. 'Is she in the D.T. ward like that guy in that film?' she said, and she giggled. 'Only I guess it'll be the women's ward.'

'I'll come along with you, Hank,' she said.

'You'll stay where you are, Mrs. Kleeber,' said Kate.

'But Hank needs somebody to go with him,' Bertha said. 'Hospitals are no place for a man.'

'Hospitals are no place for nobody,' Kate said. 'If anybody goes with Hank, I go.'

'Okay, okay.' Bertha sat down again and gave her hat another tweak to the side. 'I was only tryin' to be matey.'

'Comes kinda natural to you, doesn't it?' Kate laughed. 'Too natural. You should curb yourself a bit, sister. It might land you in trouble one of these days.'

'Comin', Hank?' she said.

In the cab she told me it was all up with Minnie. She'd had a seizure while having her hair permed. 'They can't do anything for her,' Kate said. 'It's gone

I Married Three Actresses

too far. Chronic alcoholism, they call it. It'll be a matter only of weeks.'

But when I saw Minnie I reckoned it'd be a matter only of hours. Poor Minnie, she was out for the count all right. All her bounce, all her verve had gone. Poor Min, she lived in a big way, but she died in a big way, too. I reckon I liked her best of all my wives. She was on the level. She liked booze and she made no bones about it. There was no going behind your back with Minnie. If you missed her you knew she was in bed with a bottle of gin.

A couple of weeks after Minnie died I married Kate. She more or less proposed to me. 'I feel it's time I took a husband,' she said.

I didn't give a hoot about leaving Gus and Bertha. They were small-fry and meant nothing in my life. But I was sore about leaving Andy. I've got a soft spot for that big tow-headed guy. And it's not only because he was the only one who stood by me at the trial.

But I was twenty-nine and I reckoned it was time I made my mark on the world. I didn't aim to spend the rest of my life going around with a three-bit band. And so maybe I married Kate because it gave me a chance to go places. She offered me a part in her play. I just had a few lines, but I had to play the piano in one scene. I reckoned it might get me somewhere. I'd always had a hankering to be an actor. Tickling the ivories in a three-piece was all right, but it didn't get you anywhere.

But marrying Kate didn't get me anywhere much either. I had my part in the play and my name was on the bills in small letters at the foot amongst the other small-part people. We hit Broadway, but it didn't make much difference to me. Except that people pointed me out as Kate's husband. That was the nearest to fame I

I Married Three Actresses

got. It's no cinch being married to a successful woman. I might as well have married the Woolworth Building.

It gave me an odd standing with the other actors. Either they were all over me, trying to get me to ask Kate for something for them. Or they high-hatted me completely.

It didn't make things any brighter to see Natasha's name in enormous letters a few blocks away. I met her one afternoon in the Waldorf. She was Mrs. Wally Coulter now and knee-deep in diamonds. 'Well, Hank,' she greeted me. 'Howdya like bein' Mr. Katherine Jassy?'

It's her I should have bumped off.

Life's a funny business. It doesn't run true to form always, like it does in the history books and the newspapers. It's not the big things that get you, it's the little things. You can take wars and things like that in your stride. It's the ordinary business of living that counts. It's not all as simple as boy meets girl, boy loves girl, boy marries girl, like it tells you in books. Maybe it is sometimes. But there's always one case in ten where it doesn't work out. Even in the other nine it isn't always what it seems to be.

That was the way it was with me and Kate.

There was an actress in the company called Joan Wendell. She had a pretty important part. She and Kate were buddies. And her name was in the next biggest letters to Kate's.

Besides being the star, Kate had produced this play. Soon after we hit Broadway, and the critics had said a few things about it, she began to make alterations in the production. Kate was very much The Star and The Producer in the theatre. It was only after I'd joined her company that I realised how she'd lowered herself by

I Married Three Actresses

hobnobbing with us vaudeville riff-raff. But that I guess was because of Minnie. Anyway, she kept everybody in the cast at a distance. There were none of these *darlings* and *dears* like there are in most theatres. Everybody was Mr. or Miss to her. Day after day we had rehearsals, going through scenes that had been done hundreds of times already. Kate sure was the dame to horse you on. She'd sit there and say: 'Just say those lines again, Mr. Jarvis,' or 'A little more movement there, if you please, Mr. Jarvis.'

Mr. Jarvis! Yeah, even though I was her husband she called me Mr like she called all the others. She never called me Hank once in the theatre.

The only exception she made was Joan. It was Joan this and Joan that. 'Joan darling, you might take those lines again,' or 'Joan, my sweet, if you'd just put a little more emphasis there it would make all the difference. What do you think, dear?'

It got me down. And it got me down more because the rest of the cast saw and heard the way she treated me. But it got me down most, I reckon, when even outside the theatre she made it plain that she'd no time for me. She was always going places with Joan. I might as well have been a piece of furniture for all the notice she took of me.

And so I took to two-timing Kate the way Natasha had two-timed me. I had to do something, and I had time on my hands. Yeah, I know, it all came out at the trial, and the dames had to give evidence. The Judge said what a heel I was, and the newspapers slammed me because of the great loss to the American stage. But as a newspaper guy I knew used to say: 'The truth ain't never so simple and bourgeois.'

I couldn't tell the truth at the trial. Not the whole

I Married Three Actresses

truth anyway. And I don't blame Joan for not telling it either. Nobody would have believed us, and the newspapers sure wouldn't have printed it. So I've just got to take the rap because people believe in things like fairies and kids growing under cabbages. The public wouldn't believe the truth if they got it. It's not their fault. They've been conditioned that way. They believe in sticking to what they read in books: boy meets girl, boy marries girl, boy kills girl.

It's a lot of boloney, and that's why I killed Kate. The newspapers said it was because she'd found I was two-timing her. Kate would have got a big laugh out of that, I guess. She didn't care how much I two-timed her. But what she did care about was that night I went home sooner than she expected.

Yeah, I married three actresses and I got a raw deal every time.

It's like I told the Judge. It's bad enough having a wife who goes after other men, bad enough having a wife who's on the booze all the time, but where it really gets you below the belt is when you've got a wife who thinks more of her women-friends.

I only gave Natasha a couple of socks. I wonder why I didn't give Kate the same. I reckon that stiletto we used as a paper-knife was lying too handy, and I'd had too much to drink.

Is it time?

Well, I've tickled the ivories, I've played the drums, and I've blown the horn in my time. But this'll be the first chance I've had to play the harp. I'm on my way, brother. Hope the current doesn't take too long to shoot through me.

CALL ME BLONDIE

THE foreman told him to paper the front room. 'I'll be up in Mrs. Pollock's if you want me,' he said. 'Mrs. Ames'll tell you how she wants that frieze.' He was going out when he stopped and said: 'Say, d'you think this dame Ames is all right?'

'How?' Mac said.

'She asked me if I was a detective.'

'Go on!' Mac said.

'Honest,' the foreman said. 'Well, you know where to get me. Happy huntin'!'

Mac got going. He'd got a piece hung when Mrs. Ames came in smoking a cigarette in a long holder. She took a packet out of her jacket-pocket.

'Smoke?' she said.

'Thanks a lot,' Mac said.

Mrs. Ames was a tall, thin woman with frizzy yellow hair, and her face was heavily powdered. She leaned against the steps while she held up the light for his cigarette, and Mac saw more than he should have seen.

'Will it take you long?' she said.

'Most of the day, I guess.'

'How're you doin' about dinner?' she said.

'I've got sandwiches with me,' Mac said.

'You can have dinner with me,' she said.

'Thanks a lot,' Mac said.

'Hubby won't be home till the end of the week,' Mrs. Ames said, 'He's travelling down Kilmarnock way.'

Call Me Blondie

She pottered around. 'Can't find much to do,' she said. 'I get lonesome when Hubby's away. Sometimes I go to the pictures in the afternoons, but it isn't the same as going with Mr. Ames.'

'What do you do with yourself at nights?' she said.

'Just moon around,' Mac said.

'I bet you don't moon around by yourself,' she said.

Mac laughed. Mrs. Ames laughed too. She leaned against the steps again, putting her chin on her arms and looking up at him. Mac didn't like the way she was looking at him, so he got down and began to trim the paper.

'What's your name?' Mrs. Ames said.

'Ask me no questions and I'll tell you no lies!' he said.

'I think I'll call you sweetheart,' she said. 'You ought to be somebody's sweetheart with a face like that.'

'Go on!' Mac said.

'You're a nice-lookin' kid,' she said. 'Hasn't anybody told you that before?'

'Sure,' Mac said. 'What way would you like the frieze, Mrs. Ames?'

'Any way you like,' she said. 'So long as I get it.'

'You can have it either this way or that way,' he said.

'What's the difference?' she said. 'So long as I get it.'

'Okay, Mrs. Ames,' he said.

'Don't call me Mrs. Ames,' she said. 'It makes me feel like a hundred. As if I were old enough to be your mother.'

Mac thought she wasn't so far wrong when she said that, but he said nothing.

'Call me Blondie,' she said.

'Okay,' Mac said.

He wished she'd go back to the kitchen and leave him

Call Me Blondie

to work in peace, but she took the dust-sheet off the sofa and sat down. 'Do you need to work so fast?' she said.

'I've got to finish this by to-night,' Mac said.

'Aw, it won't take you all day,' she said. 'C'mon and sit down and let's talk.'

'I've got to get this piece hung before the paste dries,' he said.

'You're a regular busy bee!' Mrs. Ames said. 'Why don't you try to make honey from somethin' sweeter than paste.'

'I know what I'm doin' with paste,' Mac said.

'Well, I guess I'll make a cup of tea,' Mrs. Ames said.

She came back with a tray and put it on a small table in front of the sofa. 'Come and sit down,' she said, patting the sofa beside her.

'Aw, jeez,' Mac said. 'My overalls'll make a mess. I'll just stand.'

'Sit down,' she said. 'I want to tell you somethin'.'

Mac sat down gingerly. 'Listen,' Mrs. Ames said. 'If you hear a ring at the door, don't answer it.'

'How?' Mac said.

She leaned forward and whispered: 'Because there're detectives after me.'

'My husband's got them trailin' me,' she said. 'He wants a divorce. He says he's away to Kilmarnock for his firm, but I know he's away with some tart. My God, I'll fix him. I'll fix them both even if I swing for it. I don't mind; I've had my fling in my time.'

'Could I have another cup of tea, please, Mrs. Ames?' Mac said.

'I thought I told you to call me Blondie,' she said.

'I forgot,' he said. 'Blondie!'

'So Hubby's got dicks trailin' me,' Mrs. Ames said.

[*82*]

Call Me Blondie

'He thinks I entertain men in here. As if I'd do such a thing. The dicks've been tryin' to get in for weeks. Sometimes they pretend they're salesmen or window-cleaners.' She stopped, her voice fading away like a radio cut-out. 'Say,' she said suddenly. 'You're not a detective, are you?'

'Do I look like a detective?' Mac said.

'If I thought you were a detective I'd stick a knife in your back,' she said.

'I'm not big enough to be a detective,' Mac said.

'No, you're not very big, are you?'

'Big enough,' he said.

'I bet you're tough,' Mrs. Ames said.

'Tough enough,' he said.

'Even the toughest guys get knocked out sometimes,' Mrs. Ames said.

'I guess so,' Mac said.

'A pinch of poison'll knock out the toughest,' she said.

'Who'd want to poison me?' Mac said.

'Well, there might be poison in that tea for all you know,' she said.

'Go on!' Mac laughed and drank the remainder of the tea quickly.

'I bet you're not afraid of anythin',' Mrs. Ames said.

'Except me,' she said, giggling.

'Go on!' Mac said.

Mrs. Ames began to edge closer to him. 'More tea?' she said.

'No, thanks,' Mac said. 'I guess I've had enough.'

He got up quickly and went on with his work. Mrs. Ames sat where she was. He wished she'd go into another room and get on with her work, but from the look of this room he guessed she didn't like work much.

'D'you ever gaze into the crystal?' Mrs. Ames said.

Call Me Blondie

'No,' Mac said. 'What'ud I want to gaze into the crystal for?'

'To see the future, of course.'

'What 'ud I want to see the future for?' he said. 'I haven't got detectives after me!'

'Wise guy!' Mrs. Ames laughed. 'I've got a crystal in the other room,' she said. 'Would you like to look into it?'

'Hell, no!' Mac said. 'I reckon you're better not to know what's comin' to you.'

'Aw, c'mon,' she said. 'It'll only take about ten minutes.'

'The foreman might come in and wonder where I was.'

'He won't be out of Mrs. Pollock's all day,' Mrs. Ames said. 'I know Mrs. Pollock.'

'I've got to hang this piece before the paste dries,' Mac said.

'You told me that before,' she said. 'C'mon.'

They went into the back bedroom. It was fairly dark, for the curtains were still drawn. The bed was unmade, but that didn't seem to worry Mrs. Ames. The crystal was on a small table. They sat facing each other, and Mrs. Ames held Mac's hands. Her knees pressed against his, and she kept on pressing and pressing until he thought she'd end up under the table. He could see nothing in the crystal.

'Doesn't this make you feel wonderful?' Mrs. Ames said.

'No,' he said. 'Why should it?'

'You haven't got a romantic nature,' she giggled. 'Now, lookit me. I've got a romantic nature, and then some.'

'Don't you believe I've got a romantic nature?' she said.

Call Me Blondie

'Sure,' Mac said, trying to wriggle his knees away from hers.

'Hubby doesn't think I've got a romantic nature,' Mrs. Ames said. 'But I'll fix him.'

'I'll fix anybody that crosses me,' she said. 'I'm a bad enemy—but I'm a good friend.'

Mac was beginning to get nervous. 'If there's nothin' in the crystal I think I'd better get back to work,' he said.

'What's your hurry?' Mrs. Ames said. 'Wait a minute.'

She peered into the crystal, holding Mac tight by the wrists. 'I see you!' she cried. 'I see you with a fair-haired girl. You're walkin' in a park and your arm's around her waist. Gee, have you fallen for her in a big way!'

'I'd better go back to work now,' Mac said.

'Just a minute,' Mrs. Ames cried. 'It's gettin' clearer. You're goin' out of the park into a wood. It's dark in that wood—darker than it is in this room. Gee, I'm so excited I can't see what's happenin'. What do *you* think's happenin', sweetheart?'

'The foreman's comin' down to see how I'm gettin' on,' Mac said. And he loosened his hands and rose. He was moving away when Mrs. Ames moaned and sagged over the crystal. Mac made a movement towards her, then he stopped. He looked at the glass jug with water beside the bed. He half moved towards it, then he shrugged and went to the door. If she really had fainted it was none of his business. He was opening the door when Mrs. Ames sat up, shrieking: 'There's somethin' terrible in that wood! Somethin' terrible's goin' to happen to you!'

But Mac didn't wait to hear what it was. He went back to the front room. He didn't see Mrs. Ames all day after that. He heard her moving about the house, but

[85]

Call Me Blondie

she never appeared. She didn't offer him any dinner, as she'd promised, but he ate his sandwiches. At night when he went back to the shop with his steps and brushes, Mr. Brownlee called him into the office.

'Mrs. Ames has just phoned, Macpherson,' he said. 'She's missed a pearl necklace.'

When they searched him they found the necklace in the inside pocket of Mac's jacket, which had been hanging all day in Mrs. Ames' hall. 'Well, what do you think of that?' Mr. Brownlee said, dangling it in front of him.

'Woolworth's,' Mac said.

'Mrs. Ames doesn't want to prosecute,' Mr. Brownlee said. 'So all I can do is give you your Books. You ought to think yourself lucky.'

'I do,' Mac said, and as he went out he said: 'Kiss Blondie good-bye for me.'

BUT GERMAN GIRLS WALK DIFFERENT

EVER since I was a kid I've been crazy about horses. I've always wanted one of my own. But there was fat chance of that, living in a tenement in Glasgow—even if the old man had had the money to buy me one. And anyway, even if the old lady hadn't cut up rough, what would the neighbours have said if I'd kept it tethered in the back-green?

When I joined the Army I fancied myself in the Guards riding one of these great shiny chargers. But the Guards were mechanised by then, and anyway I wasn't big enough to be a Guardsman. So I just had to go into the bleeding infantry. And all I want now is to get demobbed and get back to Civvy Street as quick as I can with Marta. There'll be ructions with the old lady about that, I guess. I don't know how kindly she'll take to a German daughter-in-law. But maybe things'll be all right. The old lady's not a bad old spud if you take her in the right way.

It's funny what three months in your life do. Three months ago there I was right in the middle of Germany, and the only things that worried me were the non-fratting and the fact that I couldn't get to ride one of the many beautiful German horses I saw. But all that was changed by Blister Hill in one night.

Blister's a Canadian who's attached to our unit. He's a great boy for *winning* things. Everything he sees that he wants he just goes and grabs, and if people complain—

But German Girls Walk Different

well, it's just too bad. Blister's 'won' it and nothing can be done.

At first Blister had several brushes with our C.O. about this. Our C.O. is a bit like a schoolmaster; that's why we christened him 'The Beak.' It started one day when a bloke came into our R.H.Q. and handed me a sheaf of papers and said: 'That's for the C.O.'

I must have looked puzzled. I was wondering what this bloke who's a truck-driver was doing with papers for the C.O. For the fellow said: 'You'll laugh when you read these. I had to laugh myself. I had my truck parked by the side of the road last night, and the old geezer himself came along and raised no end of a stink. "Don't you know it's illegal to park an army vehicle by the roadside, my man?" he says. "Write out one hundred times *It is a punishable offence to park an army vehicle by the side of a road*, and bring it to my office in the morning."'

'I sat up half the night doing them,' the bloke said. 'Don't laugh, will you?'

But it was no laughing matter. As that guy on the radio says: 'It makes you think!' Anyway, it made some of our blokes think, and it helped a lot when some of them who didn't know what their politics were put in their votes at the election.

Blister, of course, is the sort of guy who knows how to vote without letting anything or anybody influence him. 'Private enterprise all the time for me,' he says. 'My own, and my friends.'

Blister took a sort of shine to me. You know how it is. He said I was such a little guy I needed protecting. 'Got to keep you from getting tied up with any of these husky German fräuleins,' he said. 'If one of them gets her talons on you, you'll be mincemeat in no time.'

And so Blister and me have palled around ever since

But German Girls Walk Different

he joined our crowd. I've learned a lot from him about winning things. I used to think I was pretty hot in the old days in Glasgow, but I knew nothing until I fell in with Blister. My old lady used to say: 'The quickness of the hand deceives the left foot!' But even that couldn't describe Blister. He leaves me dizzy. I've often said to him it's not right to win things off people the way he does. 'Even though they are Jerries!' I've said.

But although he's left me dizzy often, he's never left me as dizzy as that night he brought me the horse.

I'd told him sometimes how I'd always wished I could have a horse and how I'd have liked to be a jockey. And I'd told him about wanting to go in the Guards and not being big enough. But I never thought it had sunk in. Two-three times he said: 'Aw, but we'll get you a horse, Chuck! We can easy win a horse. Leave that to your Uncle Blis!' But I never cottoned on to it much. I just thought he was talking big in his own Canadian way.

And then one night he came into our billet grinning all over. 'Get your boots on, brother!' he said. 'Get on your boots and bring your saddle! We're gonna ride the range to-night! Yippee!'

'Ach, I'm no' goin' oot the night,' I said. 'I'm ower tired, and I cannie be fashed.'

'Come on!' he cried. 'There ain't gonna be no empty saddles in the old corral to-night! Get booted and spurred. We're gonna roam the range together!'

'I dinnie want to go oot,' I said.

But he took hold of me and put my boots on, then he picked me up and carried me out. And all the time he kept singing a lot of cowboy songs. He caused such a commotion that the rest of the chaps in the billet came along to see what was up.

But German Girls Walk Different

And like me they nearly passed out when they saw the horse. It was a black German cavalry horse: a super bit of work.

'Well, what do you think of Old Faithful, chum?' Blister said, unhitching it from a post and leading it up to me. 'Will he suit your nibs?'

'Where'd ye get him?' I said.

Blister shrugged and patted the horse's neck. 'I won him,' he said.

'But ye cannie win a horse,' I said. 'No' a horse o' this size, anyway!'

'I was walking in the country,' Blister said. 'And as I walked along I passed a field where this horse was grazing. Now, horses are very inquisitive animals. As soon as this horse saw me, it galloped up and nodded to me over the fence. So I nodded back and said: 'How do, old fella!' Well, I walked along, and the horse walked along beside me. Then we came to a gate. So I leaned on the gate, and as I was leaning I thought about you, kid, and how you'd always wanted a horse, and I said to myself: 'Blister, it ain't good for that kid to go on wanting a horse that bad. It's bad for his psychology, Blister,' I says. 'Frustration and all that.' And I was so busy thinking all this I didn't notice what my hand was doing, but it must have been playing with the latch of the gate, for when I started to walk away I discovered that the horse had nosed open the gate and was following me. The Pied Piper!'

'He's a nice horse,' he said.

'He's a nice horse sure enough,' I said. 'But—oh, it's an awful big But! What are we goin' to do with him? We cannie hide a horse like we could hide a blanket or a chicken or a keg o' rum.'

'Ye'll have to take him back, Blister,' I said.

But German Girls Walk Different

'Can't, buddy,' he said. 'I couldn't find his field now even if you paid me!'

'He's yours now,' he said. 'You won him. C'mon, get on his back.' And before I knew where I was he'd lifted me on the horse.

For the next two-three minutes I hadn't time to think of anything but keeping myself from sliding off the horse's back. Blister, of course, had forgotten to win a saddle—though he'd gotten a bridle all right. And all the time I kept thinking about the Beak and about him making inquiries, and about where we were to hide the horse. You see, you can hardly hide a horse under your bed. Not a horse of this size, anyway.

I said this to Blister after I'd galloped two-three times up and down the lane beside our billet. I was all for taking the horse back, and so were the other chaps. But Blister was stubborn. There's a bit of the mule about Blister; maybe that's why the horse took to him. 'We'll put him in the old Frau's washing-house at the foot of the garden,' he said. 'For to-night, anyway. We'll decide what to do about him to-morrow.'

The other chaps were up in arms about this. Frau Gottlieb wasn't a bad old kipper, but she could be a holy terror when roused; and they all thought a great muckle horse amongst her washing would be just the thing to make her rush straight to the Beak. And so we had a great discussion. Some of the fellows, like me, were all for turning the horse loose and letting it find its own way back to its field. But Blister said, 'It's goin' into the old Frau's wash-house.'

I argued and argued with him while we were doing this, telling him we'd have the Beak down on us like a load of bricks. 'It's all very well winning a rug or a bottle of whisky,' I said. 'But a great muckle horse is

But German Girls Walk Different

a different matter. How do ye expect me to take it hame to Glesca? I couldnie very well hide it in ma kitbag, could I? Just you picture me walkin' doon the gang-plank off the leave-boat with that horse on ma back!'

I never slept that night for worrying. And the next morning we had a round-table discussion about it while we were shaving in the wash-house. One of the lads had aye to be standing at the door, keeking to see that Frau Gottlieb wasn't coming. But luckily she never appeared.

Blister was still stubborn. 'I won't take him back,' he said. 'He followed me here. He likes me, don't you, old boy?' And he nodded to the horse and winked, and the bloody horse neighed back at him. 'I tell you what,' Blister said. 'We'll leave the decision until after breakfast. I'll lock the wash-house door and put the key in my pocket, so the old Frau won't be able to find out. Maybe the Lord will be on our side and solve the problem for us.'

But the Lord must have slept late that morning, for after breakfast we were called on parade, and there was the C.O. with an old Jerry farmer and a young girl who spoke some English. My knees were knocking together, but I couldn't keep my eyes offen this dame. She was the classiest bit of work I'd seen since I came to Germany. All the time the Beak was talking I watched her. I was so busy watching that I scarcely heard the Beak say that if the horse wasn't returned he'd make every man-jack in the unit write out a thousand times *Thou Shalt Not Steal*. And as I watched her I suddenly thought of a wonderful scheme. I saw it all in a flash. Me and Blister would take the horse back to their farm and we'd say we'd found it wandering on the road, and then the old guy and his daughter would fall on our necks and hail

But German Girls Walk Different

us as conquering heroes and whatnot, and then—domino!—the girl would fall for me.

But I'd reckoned again without Blister, for when I looked for him after parade he was nowhere to be seen. And when I went to the wash-house the door was open and the horse gone.

Blister came back about an hour later and said: 'Well, I've done it. I couldn't bear the thought of writing that thing out a thousand times. Hope you're satisfied, buddy.'

I could have killed him. I told him what I'd been planning, and then I said: 'But now ye've ruined it, you—you big cheese!'

Blister said nothing, and he kept out of my way all that day. I looked for him after supper, for I wanted to know where this girl's farm was; I thought maybe he and I could walk along there and maybe we'd see the girl and then, maybe, with Blister to give me courage, I'd be able to speak to her. But Blister was nowhere to be seen, and he didn't appear until just before lights out. He stood inside the door and beckoned me. 'Come here, you,' he said, jerking his thumb outside. 'This what you want?'

The horse was tethered to the wash-house door.

Well, to cut a long story short, there was the same pantomime the next morning with the old Jerry farmer and his daughter at our Beak, looking again for their horse. But after it me and Blister got busy. We nipped over to the wash-house and took the horse to the farm. 'We found him wandering on the road,' Blister said. 'You should lock him up more carefully, mister. Lots of them soldiers aren't to be trusted.'

The old farmer almost fell on our necks. He couldn't do enough to entertain us, and speaking for myself I

But German Girls Walk Different

was perfectly willing to stay in his comfortable farm-kitchen as long as it was Marta who was pouring out the wine and handling round cakes.

I was still dizzy as we walked back to our billet. But Blister was kinda moody. He said nothing all the way except to tell me to stop acting like a kid when I gave two-three hop-skips and a jump. 'This love business!' he said.

I didn't answer, but just after that when we passed a couple of Yankee soldiers and I heard one of them say: 'But German girls walk different,' I nudged him and said: 'D'ye hear that, chum? Doesn't that prove things to you?'

'I heard,' he said. And then he sighed and said: 'He was an awful nice horse.'

All the same, it looks now the way things are panning out that maybe I'll get the horse as well as Marta, for the old farmer said to me only yesterday that he would give us the horse as a wedding-present. But I'm not so sure about that. It will maybe be hard enough going with the old lady if I take home Marta without having the horse thrown in.

THE DREAM BOOK

BETTY had been only a few days in the job before she discovered that *The Dream Book* was one of the most important things in the office. For years a long line of typists had consulted it, making it dirty and dog-eared. But although many of its pages were loose, only one of them was missing. This was because a certain Miss Jenny Grey had had a particularly horrible dream about cats, and she had been in such a fury at its meaning that she had torn out the page and burned it. 'Every girl who's worked here since could cheerfully have strangled Miss Jenny Grey,' Marjorie told Betty. 'I've often wanted to do it myself.'

The idea of Marjorie trying to strangle anybody amused Betty, for Marjorie was small and delicate-looking, with long ash-blonde hair which she wore swept up in the fashionable Edwardian style.

On Betty's second Monday morning Marjorie rushed in and did not take time to go to The Boudoir with her hat and coat. She turned over the pages of *The Dream Book* with nervous fingers.

Betty stopped oiling her typewriter and watched her. As usual, Marjorie was dressed with a smartness that Betty was dying to emulate. She sighed as she took in the line of Marjorie's new pale green coat, wishing her mother would allow her to choose her own clothes and not always buy things that she said were 'sensible.'

Miss Helen Blyth, who was taking the cover off her

The Dream Book

typewriter, smiled sardonically at Marjorie and said: 'You shouldn't take chips for supper, dearie!'

'I beg your pardon,' Marjorie said. 'I was at the Dove's Nest last night and had something a lot more classy than chips.'

'The Dove's Nest?' Betty said. 'Where's that?'

Marjorie and Helen looked at each other and smiled pityingly. 'Little girls should be seen and not heard,' Miss Blyth said.

'It's the new road-house at Colinton,' Marjorie said.

There was a guffaw from Craig, the junior clerk. He winked at Betty and said: 'In other words, Toots, it's a pub!'

'I beg your pardon,' Marjorie said grandly. 'You can get supper or anything else you want there. You don't need to go into the bar at all.' She giggled. 'The boy-friend and I had an awful laugh when we were there. You'd have died! We were in the middle of supper when two old hags peered in the door.'

'Vigilantes!' Craig said.

'That's what we thought, too,' Marjorie said. 'But when they saw the coast was clear they came in and said to the waitress: 'The usual, please.'

Betty sighed enviously. Helen and Marjorie had ever so much fun. They went to places she'd sometimes never even heard about. Marjorie's boy-friend, Stuart, took her to cafés or pictures nearly every night, and Helen had a lot of gentlemen-friends who took her to posh places like the North British and the Caley. Helen had been in the Pompadour Restaurant once when Anton Dolin was there, and she'd been in the Mandrake Club once before it was raided. Ever since then Craig had chaffed her, asking if the proprietor hadn't wanted 'to book her out.' Betty wished she could answer Craig in

The Dream Book

the way Helen and Marjorie answered. They met his wisecracks with wisecracks, but if they got really annoyed at him they said they'd give him a thick ear and then he'd shut up. But Betty could never find an answer for him when he jibed at her gawkiness and lack of sophistication; she just had to smile and pretend she was enjoying his nonsense. Of course, she told herself, by the time she was as old as Marjorie and Helen she'd be capable of dealing with his rudeness as well as they did. For both Marjorie and Helen were ever so old—Marjorie was twenty-five, and Helen *said* she was twenty-seven. Each of them had successfully modelled herself on her favourite film star. Marjorie was ever so refined really, and at a distance she might easily be mistaken for Betty Grable, but occasionally when she wisecracked with Craig she was just a little bit vulgar—oh, ever so little, of course. But Helen was ever so hard-boiled and she nearly always was vulgar. All the same she looked ever so much more like a lady than Marjorie did. Helen was stately.

Betty wondered if she'd ever be like them. She had a favourite film star, too—Lana Turner—but somehow or other she never was able to say and do the things Lana said and did. When she tried, Dick always got annoyed and said: 'Really, you should see yourself, kid!'

Dick was ever so nice, of course, and she liked him a lot, but that was no excuse for him to say things like that. It wasn't as if he were her regular boy-friend like Marjorie's Stuart. He took her out only on Saturday nights to the flicks and sometimes for a walk on Sundays. She knew he couldn't afford to take her to the places where Stuart took Marjorie, but if only he'd take her out more often she'd be pleased. Most nights, though, he preferred to go with his chums, and she was forced

The Dream Book

to fall back on her girl-friend for company. Ella wasn't any too pleased about it. 'Just making me a stand-in!' she said. She said, too, that boys were all alike; they wanted you only when their chums had nothing else on. Ella had had a few boy-friends and she knew.

Marjorie flung down *The Dream Book* and cried: 'Damn that woman Grey!'

'C?' Helen said.

'Yeah, I had a dream about clouds. Black clouds.'

'That's trouble, dearie. You don't need a dream book for that,' Miss Blyth said. 'What was the rest of the dream about?'

'I was digging in the garden,' Marjorie said.

'It must have been a dream!' Craig said.

'And I dug up a lot of worms,' Marjorie said, looking at Craig as if he were one.

'Worms?' Helen said. 'Look it up.'

'Worms,' Marjorie read. 'To dream of worms foretells news of the death of somebody near and dear to you.' She paused. 'Gee, I wonder who that can be?'

'The cat!' Craig grinned.

'The mater was complaining about her back yesterday,' Marjorie said. 'But that was only a gag. She wanted me to polish the linoleum in the hall. She said it couldn't wait until the char came on Wednesday. . . .

'The pater's all right,' she mused, flicking through the pages of *The Dream Book* as if for further guidance. 'Nothing's ever wrong with the pater unless he loses at golf. . . . And Stuart's okay—unless he's going to have an accident with his old mo'-bike.'

'Don't worry, dearie,' Helen said. 'Stuart's not such a damned fool.'

'Uncle Bill wasn't very well last week,' Marjorie said. 'He had a rotten cold. It was nothing serious . . . but

The Dream Book

still you never know with a cold. It might develop into pneumonia or something. . . . Maybe it'll be him.'

'Maybe,' Helen said hopefully.

'D'you think I'd need to wear black?' Marjorie said. 'After all, he's not really a blood relation. Aunt Alice is the pater's sister. D'you think my black hat would do? I could take off the green ornament.'

'Search me,' Helen said, yawning.

'Come into The Boudoir and I'll oblige!' Craig said.

'Smart guy!' Helen said. 'What did *you* dream about last night?'

'You're too young to hear,' Craig said. 'Ask Jack the Ripper.' He indicated the office-boy, who was listening with goggling eyes. 'He should have something ripe to tell!'

The office-boy blushed.

This morning at ten Betty was to take dictation from young Mr. Miles Johnstone. It had been Helen's job, but on Friday Mr. Miles had asked for Betty. Her shorthand was fairly good, but she was so nervous that she didn't get the first few letters down properly. Because she had a good memory, however, and because most of Mr. Miles' letters were couched in the same trite terms, she had managed to type them all right. She was annoyed at her nervousness. She had never been nervous when taking dictation at night school, and the teacher dictated much more quickly than Mr. Miles. She dismissed the idea that it was because the night-school teacher was middle-aged and bald. Old Mr. Johnstone was middle-aged and bald, too, but if she had to take dictation from him she'd be simply terrified. But Mr. Miles was ever so nice and ever so friendly—not like a boss at all! Marjorie and Helen referred to him as 'Big Boy,' and Betty

The Dream Book

suspected they called him that to his face. She wasn't sure, but she thought that both of them had been out with him at different times.

This morning Mr. Miles had only a few letters, and he didn't seem to know what to say in them. Betty sat expectantly with her pencil poised. So far she had got down every word. She noticed that Mr. Miles was staring at her ankles, and she wished that she was wearing cute fully-fashioned silk stockings like Marjorie instead of the lisle-thread ones her mother had bought for her. To try to forget them, she began to compare Mr. Miles with Dick. To Dick's disadvantage. After a few seconds of this, she became ashamed of herself. After all, Dick couldn't help it if he hadn't been educated at a public school and a university. He really was as good-looking as Mr. Miles, only—well, they were what you might call different types of male beauty. Dick was just the least little bit common-looking—oh, ever so little, of course. Her parents thought he was ever so tall, but she knew he'd look insignificant beside Mr. Miles. She guessed Dick would say Mr. Miles was beefy and that his head was as thick as his legs, but she was prepared to defend Mr. Miles against any criticism. Of course, Dick was only nineteen—a year older than herself. People said you grew until you were twenty-five, but somehow or other she didn't think Dick would ever be as tall or as broad as Mr. Miles even though he lived to be a hundred.

Mr. Miles played rugby—no, she must remember to call it rugger as Marjorie had told her. Rugger was the right word. Stuart had told Marjorie it was 'the done thing.' Betty was glad she wasn't a rugger-player. She wouldn't like to be tackled and knocked down by Mr. Miles' heavy body. . . . She became so confused at the

The Dream Book

cavalcade of fancies that coursed through her consciousness that she didn't hear one word of Mr. Miles' next sentence.

'Pardon?' she said, remembering that Marjorie had told her to say this always and never 'I beg your pardon.' Marjorie said that only when she was being sarcastic.

'Have you got that Monday-morning feeling, too, Miss Petrie?' Mr. Miles laughed.

'I—I'm sorry,' Betty said.

'It's all right,' Mr. Miles said. 'I guess we're both in the same boat. What we need is a tonic! A visit to the Dove's Nest or some place exciting like that.'

Betty twiddled nervously with her pencil. Mr. Miles rose and stretched himself until she began to think his huge body would burst through his expensive suit. He stood beside her chair, smiling down at her. There was a glint of gold on one of the even white teeth beneath his small dark moustache.

'How about it?' he said.

'I—I really couldn't,' she said.

She stood up, trembling violently because of his nearness.

'Why not?' he said softly, and he put his arm around her waist. 'You're not afraid of me, are you?'

'Of course not,' she said.

'Tell me another!' he grinned.

'I'm not,' she said.

'Then you'll meet me to-night at eight?'

'No,' she said.

'Why not?'

'I'm going out to-night,' she lied.

'To-morrow night then?' he said.

She shook her head, but he said: 'To-morrow at

The Dream Book

eight. You'll tell me definitely to-morrow morning, won't you?'

She felt so queer when she returned to the outer office that she paid three visits to The Boudoir in less than an hour.

'What's wrong, dearie?' Helen said. 'Been takin' medicine?'

Betty would gladly have sent flowers to Miss Blyth's funeral at that moment, but at lunch-time Helen said: 'Don't mind me, dearie. You ought to know me better by this time. Was Big Boy up to some of his tricks this morning?'

Betty blushed, but before she could say anything Helen said: 'Watch your step with that big gorilla, dearie. I nearly missed mine.'

All afternoon and evening Helen's advice rankled in Betty's mind. What right had Helen to tell her what to do? Maybe she was afraid she would queer her pitch. Come to think of it, she had superseded Helen as Mr. Miles' typist. . . . Well, she'd show Miss Blyth she wasn't the only one who could go to posh places with gentlemen friends. . . . But what about her parents? They were dreadfully old-fashioned in some of their ideas. They thought that typists who went out with their bosses were no good. They'd think she was heading for the downward path. . . . Going out with Dick was different. You were safe in the ninepenny seats of the cinema — especially when you paid your own way!

Oh, if only she had somebody to advise her. . . .

On Tuesday morning Betty grabbed *The Dream Book* as soon as she came in. As she frantically turned the pages Helen and Craig winked to each other. 'Well, dearie?' Helen said.

The Dream Book

'I dreamed I was riding a horse through a field of ripe corn,' Betty said.

'Weren't you scared to death?' Helen said. 'I know I'd have been. I'm terrified if a horse even looks at me.'

'But not as frightened as the horse when it sees you looking at it,' Craig said.

'Horses. To dream of horses is very good,' Betty read. 'You are going to change your station in life.'

'You'll get out at Blackhall instead of Murrayfield,' Craig said.

'Corn?' Betty said, turning the pages. 'Oh, damn Miss Jenny Grey! What's another word for corn?'

'A bunion,' Craig said.

'Very poor, dear. I'm afraid you're losing your touch,' Helen said. 'Try grain, dearie,' she said to Betty.

'To dream of grain foretells riches and that you are going to reap your desires,' Betty read. 'Gee, don't you think the combination of the two things is symbolic?'

'Carbolic you mean,' Craig said.

'That's what you need,' Helen said. She looked reflectively at Betty. 'Don't put your faith in that twaddle,' she said. 'Remember what I told you.'

'What's wrong with you this morning?' Craig said to Helen. 'Aren't you going to consult Madame Verbena?'

'I slept like a log last night, dearie,' Helen said.

'You don't need to go to bed to do that,' he grinned.

'No, I get nightmares all day here looking at you!'

Betty began to dust her desk. It was all a lot of nonsense of course. She was silly to have gone as far as consult the book. She'd better take Helen's advice. If ever she went to the Dove's Nest it would be with Dick, or somebody like him. Still . . . it would be sort of nice to go with Mr. Miles. Just once anyway. There wasn't any harm in that. It wasn't as if she didn't like him. In a

The Dream Book

way she liked him better than she liked Dick. It was only that she'd known Dick longer. If only you could believe in *The Dream Book*. . . .

Marjorie burst in breathlessly. She was wearing her black hat. The green ornament had disappeared from it.

'Oh, girls!' she cried.

'Your Uncle Bill, dearie?' Helen said.

'Oh, him!' Marjorie said. 'No, he's all right as far as I know or care. It's Tiger! He got run over by a car last night.'

'Tough luck, dearie,' Helen said, patting Marjorie's shoulder as she passed on her way to The Boudoir.

Betty shivered apprehensively. Tiger was only a dog, of course, but after all *The Dream Book* HAD said someone near and dear. She shook out the duster that she had just folded and she began to dust her desk again.

'I think this is a Bad Man,' Helen cried, waving an order that had come in.

'You should know,' Craig said. 'You've seen plenty.'

'But you're the worst!' Miss Blyth said.

As she began to search in the filing cabinet, to see if her supposition was correct, Helen hummed: 'Do not trust him, do not trust him, gentle maiden. . . .'

Betty looked venomously at her, and she laid out her pencil and notebook in readiness for going into Mr. Miles' room. She had made up her mind. She would go with him to the Dove's Nest. Once anyway, just to see what it was like. . . . Surely there was no harm in going once?

THE JOLLY GARÇON

WHEN Miss Violet Ewart was forty she retired from the stage. A legacy from an aunt made this possible. Miss Ewart's heart was not really in the stage anyway. Her doting parents had sent her to R.A.D.A. and ever since she graduated she had appeared in a series of highbrow plays. Critics said her Medea and her Lady Teazle were performances to be remembered. But Miss Ewart herself was tired of appearing in Sunday-night performances at half-empty Little Theatres, or in distinguished plays which had only short runs in the West End. The trouble with Miss Ewart was that she was much too intelligent to be a successful actress. She would never have deigned to act in most of the trashy plays that managers and agents submitted to her. She had a small and loyal, though very highbrow, following, but as she said to her friend and companion, Miss Buchanan: 'This isn't enough. I'm tired of being a Nora slamming the door of her cardboard Doll's House behind her. I want the final curtain to come down with me safely clasped in the arms of a strong silent man.'

Miss Buchanan pursed her lips thoughtfully and said: 'But you know, darling, that there are no strong silent men in the theatre.'

Miss Ewart knew this even better than her friend, but she wailed: 'I want romance, damn it, I want old-fashioned love!'

Miss Buchanan sighed. Nobody knew better of the dearth of romance than she did. For, after all, for more

The Jolly Garçon

years than she cared to remember she had helped to purvey it. She wrote love-stories for popular women's papers and made quite a tidy income from the frustration and wish-fulfilment of millions of women.

'You'd be a fool to leave the stage, Vi,' she said. 'Especially when you've got as far as you have. Think, darling, you might become another Marie Tempest yet.'

'Yeah, and look at what happened to her!' Miss Ewart said. 'No, thank you, Bucky, I'm not having malicious friends saying—"Full house as usual!"—at *my* funeral.'

And so when her aunt died and left her the money Miss Ewart retired immediately. She had been hoping for her aunt's death, banking on the legacy. But what she had not banked upon was the possession of a windmill in the village of Pomfret Pond. This was a complete surprise. Her aunt had bought it just before her death.

'We'll go and live in it,' she cried. 'A windmill! I've always wanted to live in a windmill. It's so romantic.'

'There'll likely be rats in it,' Miss Buchanan said morosely. 'There's bound to be. Just wait and see.'

'Don't be so pessimistically Scotch,' Violet said.

'Scots,' Miss Buchanan said. 'Or Scottish.'

'Well, be pedantic if you must,' Miss Ewart said. 'But don't be pessimistic. I know I'm going to adore living in a windmill.'

'Though I wish it had been a lighthouse,' she said. 'I've always wanted to live in a lighthouse.'

'You're just thinking of the sailors that might be wrecked on the rocks,' Miss Buchanan said.

'Still, the windmill's sails might catch something else,' Violet said. 'We'll go and live in it, anyway.'

Miss Buchanan agreed unwillingly. She hated to leave their flat in Hampstead, and she hated even more to give up the company and so-called friendship of the

The Jolly Garçon

young men who were always being psycho-analysed and the young women who took drugs. Miss Buchanan got quite a kick out of hearing their tales of woe and their boastings about bed.

'And material!' she said to Miss Ewart. 'Where am I going to get the material for my stories now?'

Miss Ewart said: 'You'll get plenty in the country, Bucky. Handsome farm-labourers and pretty milk-maids. I'm quite looking forward to them.'

She then said that she would revert to her baptismal name of Stubbings. 'I don't want to be bothered with people staring at me because I'm an actress,' she said. 'And I really couldn't bear stupid school-children asking for my autograph.'

Miss Buchanan said nothing; she hardly thought that any of the inhabitants of Pomfret Pond would ever have heard of Miss Ewart, far less been to the Arts or the New Lindsey, or even to any of the West End theatres to see her.

'And it sounds so respectable,' Miss Ewart said.

Again Miss Buchanan held her tongue. She did not like to tell her friend that nobody would ever have taken her for other than a West End tart.

'I might even buy a wedding-ring and call myself Mrs. Stubbings,' Miss Ewart said.

Miss Buchanan felt she had to say something about this. 'But you don't look married, Vi,' she cried. 'Even after all those men in your life!'

This led to a long argument, but finally Miss Ewart agreed to meet her friend half-way. It was as Miss Stubbings and Miss Buchanan, therefore, that they reached the village of Pomfret Pond, after the windmill had been made habitable. At first Miss Stubbings assumed a hunted look whenever one of the villagers

The Jolly Garçon

stared at her. But as none of them asked for autographs and nobody mentioned the stage she realised that her identity was a complete secret. Miss Buchanan had no such fears. She knew she was hardly likely to be taken for the glamorous Poppy de Silver, who got hundreds of fan-letters from young women, asking for advice about their romantic tangles. She was very glad that she'd arranged with her publishers to send these letters only once a week in a registered parcel addressed to Miss Robina Buchanan. She knew what local postmen were, and she was determined that her stocky tweed-clad figure was not to be allowed to destroy any illusions amongst Poppy's readers in Pomfret Pond.

After the first week of moving in, their life in the windmill was uneventful. Every morning Miss Buchanan sat at her typewriter and pounded out her thousand words of romance and heart-throbs. Every morning Miss Stubbings took the dogs for a walk, after chatting with the village woman who came to 'do' for them. And every afternoon the two ladies sat in the garden. Miss Buchanan dozed and wondered how Arthur was getting on with his guardsmen and whether Tilly had stopped taking drugs yet. And Miss Stubbings read *The Stage* or the latest highbrow novel.

Every evening the two ladies walked a quarter of a mile across the common to the local pub, 'The Bugler's Call.' Miss Stubbings needed her three gins, and Miss Buchanan her forty cigarettes. 'God knows what'll happen if the pub fails me some night,' she said. 'The grocer won't ever give me any, and it's no use trying the shops in Aylesbury. They just stare, as if a woman like me had no right to smoke. I really think sometimes that I'll have to ask Tilly to send me some drugs.'

They were ignored by the local gentry, and the

The Jolly Garçon

villagers were too much in awe to do more than return their good-mornings and good-nights. They were a curious-looking couple. Miss Stubbings was tall and willowy, heavily painted and addicted to loose flowing gowns; Miss Buchanan was short and stout, severely dressed, and her hair was shorter than some men's.

In the pub nobody but the publican and his wife spoke to them. They did their best to be matey, but they were left alone to sit stolidly and talk to each other about Tilly and Arthur and dear Bertie Winthrop's new play. They eyed the people playing darts, but they were never asked to join the game.

'What a God-awful lot of people,' Violet said one evening. 'They look quite moronic.'

'Of course, all English villages are like this,' she said. 'It's all the in-breeding that goes on.'

'Well now, I must say it's not so bad in Scotland,' Miss Buchanan said. 'There really are some fine-looking people in some Scottish villages.'

'Now, Bucky!' Violet cried. 'Don't go all Scots Nationalist on me. After all you've said against Scotland in the past!'

'I know I hate the place,' Miss Buchanan said. 'Still——'

'You haven't been there for twenty years,' Miss Stubbings said. 'How do you know that they're full of fine-looking people? They're probably all morons, too, by this time.'

'Well, after all those Poles and whatnots that were around during the War,' Miss Buchanan conceded.

They had been there almost a month when Violet said: 'Really, I'm getting quite sick of the sight of the people in that pub. They depress me. I don't think I'll go to-night.'

The Jolly Garçon

'Well, I'm going,' Miss Buchanan said. 'I need my fags.'

'Only one gin then,' Violet said. 'I really couldn't stay and drink any more.'

It was early and few of the regulars had arrived yet. Miss Stubbings and Miss Buchanan sat in a corner where they could see everything without being seen too much themselves. Miss Buchanan was gazing into her gin, working out the plot of Poppy de Silver's latest story, when Violet gave her a violent nudge. 'What a pretty boy!' she hissed.

It was a young soldier. He was about medium height, well built, with burnished copper-coloured hair. His good-looking face was tanned a deep brown.

'Not bad,' Miss Buchanan said. 'Though I'd never make him top of the bill.'

'Not bad!' Miss Stubbings said. 'I think he's wonderful.'

Miss Buchanan looked again, then she looked at her gin.

'He isn't bad-looking,' she said. 'But you'd never look twice at him in Piccadilly, ducky.'

'Georgeous beast!' Violet breathed.

Miss Buchanan's mind returned to her plot, though she was aware that Miss Stubbings was watching every move the soldier made. 'Don't stare so much, ducky,' she whispered. 'You'll make the poor boy self-conscious.'

The soldier was with another young man: a swarthy, burly type, wearing a nigger-brown suit with very wide trousers. Miss Buchanan at once labelled him as a gipsy, wondering if she could possibly work him into her latest story. Each of the young men was very much aware of Miss Stubbings' interest, but the gipsy did his best to ignore it and went on talking. He looked several

The Jolly Garçon

years older than the soldier. Miss Buchanan, wise and sophisticated Bohemian, made up her mind about them at once.

She finished her third gin. 'Well, will we go?' she said.

Miss Stubbings unwillingly looked away from the soldier. 'No, let's have another,' she said.

Miss Buchanan pursed her lips. Three gins was their usual. 'But why?' she said.

Miss Stubbings did not answer; almost forcibly she took Miss Buchanan's glass and darted to the bar. Bucky sighed, thinking she hadn't seen Violet in such a state since the appearance of Gerry Kinnaird ten—well, no, it must be fifteen—years ago.

'I don't really want it,' she muttered when Violet came back. 'You know that three is just enough for me.'

'Drink it slowly,' Violet hissed. 'Try to make it spin out until closing-time.'

Miss Buchanan sighed again. You couldn't do anything with Violet when she got into this state. 'Darling, don't be silly,' she said, knowing it was hopeless. 'How are you going to manage to speak to him? And even if you do, what can you do about it? You know what these small places are like.'

'I'll manage somehow,' Violet said.

But she didn't. She stared at the young man all evening, but somehow or other the gipsy always seemed to get his broad back between her and his companion. And at closing-time they left, shouting a general goodnight, but not looking in the ladies' direction.

'You've had it, chum!' Miss Buchanan said, rising unsteadily. 'Come on, let's get home.'

All the way Violet talked about the soldier. 'He really was a very pretty boy,' she kept saying every second sentence. 'I wonder where he comes from?'

The Jolly Garçon

'I don't know,' Bucky said. 'But I know where I'm going as soon as we get inside!'

The following evening Miss Stubbings couldn't go to the pub early enough. Miss Buchanan was intensely annoyed. She'd had a headache all morning, and as a result only five hundred words of Poppy's latest heart-throbs had got down on paper, and she felt that they'd need to be rewritten.

But she brightened when they reached the pub and found the soldier and the gipsyish young man already there. Violet could hardly ask coherently for two gins; she was so busy looking at them. Bucky smiled ironically and told herself she must study this from a professional viewpoint. The ghost of Poppy de Silver hovered around her.

But as the evening wore on, and she consumed more and more gin, Poppy's ghost gradually disappeared. The two young men remained aloof and inaccessible. The gipsy played darts, and the soldier talked to an old man in breeches, who had a gold ring in one ear, buying him drink after drink. Every time he passed the ladies on his way to the bar he eyed them from under his long lashes, but he never even smiled. Bucky was horrified to discover herself staring at him almost as frenziedly as Miss Stubbings.

'I don't like the look of that gipsy,' she muttered.

'There's something sinister about him,' Violet said. 'He's the kind who'd stick a knife in your back some dark night on the common.'

'He's got a hold on the pretty boy,' Bucky said.

This belief gained ground when the gipsy left off playing darts, tapped the soldier on the arm, and they both left, shouting a general good-night.

'What did I tell you?' Bucky said, as the two ladies

The Jolly Garçon

made their way unsteadily across the common. 'That gipsy has him in his power. There's something very sinister about it.'

'Don't be so Poppyish, darling,' Miss Stubbings said, recovering slightly in the cold night air. 'Don't tell me you're going to turn into one of your own most ardent readers!'

'I'm telling you,' Bucky said gruffly, spoiling it a second later, however, by belching. 'There's all sorts of queer things go on in this village. It's the border-line country, you know. In the olden days it used to be the resort of highwaymen and criminals fleeing from justice. Mrs. Dagnall in the pub told me it was a sort of No-Man's Land. The Law couldn't touch anybody who settled here.'

'Seems you and I have come to the right place then!' Vi giggled.

'At the rate you're going I should think the Law won't be long in stepping in,' Bucky said majestically. 'Cradle-snatching, that's what it is!'

'He's such a pretty boy,' Vi said.

'Yes, ducky, but there's the gipsy to be contended with!' Miss Buchanan giggled and hiccoughed. 'The gipsy's warned him, my pet! Do not trust her, pretty bo-oy, though her hair is peroxide blonde!'

'I bet all sorts of funny things go on,' she said a moment later. 'It's still got a No-Man's Landish look about it. I shouldn't be surprised to hear about incest and all sorts of queer goings-on.'

'Bucky darling!'

'That's why the people look so queer,' Miss Buchanan went on. 'They're the offspring of outlaws.'

She enlarged upon this theme. It and the Pretty Boy and the gipsy became the subject of most of their con-

The Jolly Garçon

versations for days on end. Every night they saw the two young men together in the pub, and every night the two ladies did their utmost to get them to speak. But always there was the same result. 'A blank, my lord, I drew a blank! I never told him of my love,' Violet intoned mournfully.

Some nights the Pretty Boy was in uniform, some nights in civvies. By listening to his conversation with the other locals the ladies managed to find out a good deal about him. He had been through the North African campaign and he'd been in Normandy. And he had just been demobbed and was enjoying himself before he took a job.

Every night before they went to 'The Bugler's Call' the two ladies would lecture each other. 'Only two drinks!' one would say. 'No more!' And then the other would say: 'And we mustn't stare! We've ruined our chances by staring so much. We've made the poor boy self-conscious. He thinks we're laughing at him and making jokes at his expense. You know how sensitive some of these village people are about townspeople like us.' But every night they forgot all their good resolutions as soon as the Pretty Boy appeared. And every night they discussed him and the gipsy as they walked back unsteadily to the windmill.

And then one night the Pretty Boy did not appear. The two ladies sat with their drinks, disconsolately sipping and eyeing the door. 'It's a Black Night,' Miss Stubbings said. 'Would you like a game of darts to cheer you up?'

'Darts!' Miss Buchanan said.

'In any case I don't need cheering up,' she said. 'You know perfectly well that it's not me who's interested in him.'

The Jolly Garçon

'We should play darts,' Miss Stubbings said. 'We really ought to interest ourselves more in the local sports. Do you realise that we're the only people who come to this pub who never play darts?'

'And cricket!' she said. 'We really must start going to the local cricket matches. That's the only way we'll get talking to the villagers. It'll show them that we're really interested in them and that we're *all right*.'

Miss Buchanan giggled into her gin.

'Or we might bring one of the dogs with us,' Miss Stubbings went on. 'A dog's always a good means of effecting an introduction. These villagers are crazy about dogs. Look at those French tarts who always take a dog around with them.'

'Honestly, Vi!' Miss Buchanan said.

Miss Stubbings tossed her head and gave all her attention to the dart-players. She smiled and nodded knowledgeably every time a high score was hit. She put on such a good act that the gold-earringed old man in breeches, who normally stared frostily at them, gave her an encouraging nod every now and then.

Suddenly Miss Buchanan nudged her and whispered: 'Lee jolly garsong!'

Miss Stubbings shuddered at her friend's French.

'He'll hear you, Bucky,' she hissed. 'After all, he's been in Normandy.'

But her horror at her friend gave place to a greater horror when she saw who was with the Pretty Boy. It was not the gipsy. It was much worse. It was a girl.

'What a dreadful-looking bit,' she said. 'Really, how could he! With that face and that figure, if he played his cards properly, he could have a flat in Mayfair.'

'Maybe he doesn't want to play cards,' Miss Buchanan said.

The Jolly Garçon

Apparently the Pretty Boy was perfectly aware of the interest he had aroused in the two ladies, though he never looked directly at them. He glanced occasionally at them from under his lashes. And he wedged the girl in a corner, talking all the time, and now and then indulging in a bit of slap-and-tickle. At one time the horse-play began to look as though it might go too far, and Mrs. Dagnall, the landlady, cried in a good-humoured way: 'Now then, Chris, this ain't the place for that! If you want to 'ave 'igh-jinks out you go to the common. There's plenty bushes there!'

'Chris!' Miss Stubbings breathed.

She took Miss Buchanan's empty glass and darted to the bar for more gin. 'It's a Black Night,' she said mournfully.

'And it'll be blacker if we drink any more gin,' Miss Buchanan said. 'I really can't hold it, Vi.'

'Drink it up,' Miss Stubbings said. 'Slowly.'

But there was no need to do that, for long before Miss Buchanan had reached the bottom of her glass the Pretty Boy and the girl went out. He pushed her in front of him and slapped her bottom as he shouted 'Good-night' to Mrs. Dagnall and the others.

* * * *

'I hate that pub,' Miss Stubbings said the following evening. 'The people there make me sick. We really must go to another. Where's this "Coach and Horses" place the postman told you about?'

'Over in that direction.' Miss Buchanan waved her hand vaguely. 'I don't really know. I only know it's about a mile from the village.'

'Anyway, I'm not going there, Vi,' she said. 'I'm going to "The Bugler's Call" to get my fags.'

The Jolly Garçon

'I couldn't bear it,' Miss Stubbings said. 'All that slap-and-tickle made me sick.'

Miss Buchanan began to hum 'Jealousy.'

'All right.' Violet rose majestically. 'But I warn you! Only one drink. If you want any more you'll have to stay and drink them yourself.'

The ladies walked to 'The Bugler's Call' in silence. It was broken only when they were about twenty yards from the door. 'What's wrong to-night?' Miss Stubbings said. 'Everything's very quiet.'

They looked at each other. For the past few weeks there had been a shortage of supply, both of beer and cigarettes. On several occasions the beer had run out long before the official hour for closing. So far, however, the ladies had always managed to get their gin; and Miss Buchanan had always got her forty cigarettes, though very often they had been slipped furtively to her by either Mr. or Mrs. Dagnall. There had been hints, too, that things would get worse. But they had not believed this. They felt certain that whether the men of Pomfret Pond got their mild-and-bitter or not, they would always get their gins-and-orange.

'Looks like another Black Night,' Miss Buchanan said.

Violet said nothing. She hurried ahead and went into the pub.

Miss Buchanan followed more slowly. She raised her eyebrows and whistled when she saw that there were scarcely more than half a dozen people in the bar. The old man in breeches was sitting in a corner, sipping lemonade. He nodded to her over the top of his glass.

'Sorry, ladies,' Mr. Dagnall said, spreading out his hands. 'We've struck a bad patch. No beer. Nothing but minerals!'

The Jolly Garçon

'Oh, my God!' Miss Stubbings sank against the bar. 'No spirits at all?'

'Nothing, madam.' He sighed.

'No cigarettes?' Miss Buchanan said.

'Not one in the house, madam,' he said.

'Oh, my God!' She leaned on the bar beside Vi.

'I don't know what things are coming to,' Mr. Dagnall said. 'Really I don't. I can never remember anything like this.'

'Nor me either,' the old gent with the earring said. 'Cor, I ain't drunk this stuff sin' I was a nipper so 'igh!'

'It's the Government, that's wot it is,' a farm-labourer said gloomily.

''Taint the Government,' said another.

It was wonderful, Miss Buchanan thought, how companions in adversity drew together. Not all the beer and merry-making in the world could have drawn those yokels and Miss Stubbings and herself together: yet here they were consoling each other about the shortage. For the first time since they'd come to Pomfret Pond Miss Buchanan really felt at home in 'The Bugler's Call.'

'Well, I suppose we'll have to have lemonade,' Miss Stubbings said.

'Guess that's all you can do, madam,' Mr. Dagnall said.

They drank their lemonade, and had a long conversation with Mr. Dagnall and the old gent in breeches about the Bad Times of the Present and the Good Old Days of the Past. The old gent was very down on 'them people wot comes 'ere in cars and drinks all the beer wot belongs to us locals. I ain't got a car. I got to walk 'ere on me own two legs. Tain't fair to us locals, is it, missie?' Miss Buchanan said it wasn't, then they said good-night.

The Jolly Garçon

Miss Buchanan looked again at the three cigarettes in her case and wondered how she was going to spin them out until morning. She must take the first bus to Aylesbury. Poppy de Silver couldn't write her thousand words to-morrow until she had her smokes.

As they were going out they met the Pretty Boy in the doorway.

'No beer and no cigarettes,' Miss Buchanan said to him before she realised what she was doing. It was only a second later that she realised, also, that he was alone.

'What!' he said.

'No beer and no cigarettes,' she said again, seeing that Miss Stubbings was speechless, and wondering at herself for being able to do something she couldn't have done even if fortified with four gins.

'God!' he said.

'That's the way I feel,' Miss Buchanan said. 'I don't mind about the drink, but I must have my fags.'

'Me too.' He grinned.

'I think you might get some at the "Coach and Horses",' he said.

'The "Coach and Horses"?' Miss Buchanan said. 'Where's that?'

'We're strangers in the neighbourhood,' Miss Stubbing said.

Miss Buchanan looked at her friend. There was such a thing as overdoing it.

'You go along to the end of the common,' he said, pointing. 'Then you go down Job's Lane. There's a stile about half-way down. Cross it and go over old Farmer Baldock's field. Then when you come on to the main road turn left and walk about a hundred yards. There's a narrow lane on your right. Go up it and——"

'God, I could never follow all that,' Miss Buchanan

The Jolly Garçon

said. 'I'm a perfect duffer at finding my way. I've no sense of direction at all.'

Miss Stubbings restrained a giggle. She remembered how once they'd been lost in Rome, but she stifled that memory and said:

'I don't suppose you'd care to show us the way, would you?' She smiled archly. 'You must be wanting a drink and cigarettes, too.'

'Okay,' he said. 'I don't mind a walk.'

Both ladies felt acutely self-conscious as they walked across the common on either side of him, but Chris talked volubly. Miss Buchanan was surprised at his chattiness. He's shy, she told herself. He's nervous of us, so he's talking a lot to cover it up.

But as they approached Job's Lane she reflected that it was amazing how one immediately seized upon a tag from a psychological treatise to explain every little incident. And she came to the conclusion that it wasn't shyness at all; it was simply that the gipsy wasn't there. Chris would be talkative no matter in what company he found himself. There wasn't an ounce of shyness in his composition.

He told them all about himself and his life in the Army. He was twenty-five and he was an electrician to trade. 'But I'm not taking a job just yet,' he said. 'I'm going to have a good time while my demob leave lasts. Me brother's always trying to find jobs for me, but I just told 'im "No job for little Chris yet", I says.'

'So you have a brother?' Miss Buchanan said.

'Yes, you must 'ave seen 'im with me,' he said. 'The dark chap I'm often in the "Bugler" with.'

'Oh, is that your brother?' Miss Stubbings said, because Miss Buchanan looked as if she were unable to open her mouth. 'He's not like you.'

The Jolly Garçon

'Takes after me dad,' Chris said. 'I takes after me mum.'

He talked about his brother and his family all the way to the 'Coach and Horses.' And he talked about his cousin. 'You must 'ave seen 'er, too,' he said. 'She was in the pub with me last night. People around 'ere don't know she's me cousin. They think I'm struck on 'er, so I've been carrying them on. Gives 'em something to talk about.'

'Yes, I—I noticed her,' Miss Stubbings said.

'She made me feel quite jealous,' Miss Buchanan said, thinking this was safe enough coming from her, and making up her mind she'd have no more to do with psychological text-books.

He grinned and said: 'Well, 'ere we are.'

They looked at each other and followed him into the pub. Shouting and laughter indicated that here was some beer anyway. Instinctively they drew together as he opened the bar-room door and ushered them in. And they drew even closer together when the first person they saw was the gipsy.

'I wished the floor would open and swallow me,' Violet told Miss Buchanan afterwards. 'My God, the look he gave me froze me to my very marrow.'

Miss Buchanan was too upset at the whole incident to tell her friend that this was a terrible cliché and that nobody of her accomplishments should ever use it. 'He froze me too,' she said.

And he must have frozen Chris. For no sooner were they in the bar than the young man's talkativeness evaporated. In the same way as the ladies drew together he drew towards his brother. 'I been showin' them the way,' he said, and then he said nothing else. He took the drink Miss Buchanan bought him, but the gipsy

The Jolly Garçon

shook his head when she asked him what he'd have. 'Got one,' he said.

Miss Buchanan and Miss Stubbings sipped their drinks and Miss Buchanan lit one of the ten Players she'd managed to get. The young men talked in undertones. Miss Buchanan strained her ears while pretending to examine the pictures on the walls of the bar, but she could not make out a word. Miss Stubbings' eyes were wide open, and she kept fluttering her lashes.

But the gipsy did not unbend. He finished his drink, then he touched Chris on the arm and said: 'Come on.'

Chris gulped down his beer, wiped his mouth, grinned awkwardly at the ladies, said 'Good-night,' and followed his brother out.

Miss Stubbings and Miss Buchanan looked at each other.

'We've had it again, chum!' Miss Buchanan said.

'It was most rude to say the least of it,' Miss Stubbings said next morning at breakfast. 'There we were—two lonely women! You would have thought that common decency would have made the P.B. walk back with us. Even though he showed us the way there, how was he to know that we'd be able to find our way back in the dark?'

'It's a good job I've a very good sense of direction,' Miss Buchanan said.

'And we stood him a drink!' Miss Stubbings said.

Miss Buchanan sighed. They'd already gone over and over the whole incident both this morning and last night. Even when Miss Stubbings had slipped on a cow-pad in Farmer Baldock's field it hadn't stopped her talking about it.

'I always said there was something sinister about that

[122]

The Jolly Garcon

gipsy,' she said now. 'He's far too knowledgeable for my taste.'

'Yes, he's liable to come up to us and say: "You two old tarts had better lay off my kid-brother,"' Miss Buchanan said.

'Really, Bucky, must you be so crude?' Violet cried.

'I've got to be crude,' Miss Buchanan said, rising as she saw the postman approach the windmill. 'If I wasn't crude myself, Poppy would have to be, and her readers wouldn't like it!'

'Though it might be a good thing for them,' she said, returning with the letters. 'Large one for you, dear,' she said, throwing a package in Miss Stubbings' lap.

'It's from Gerry,' Miss Stubbings said. 'The monster's sent me a play! And I've told him never to send me anything again. He won't believe I've finished with the stage.'

'Better read it, dear,' Miss Buchanan said, without looking up from her letters.

'I'll do no such thing,' Violet said. 'I'll send it straight back.'

'I wonder if the P.B's an illegitimate child?' she said a few moments later. 'He's so different from his brother. I wouldn't mind betting that he's the son of the local squire. You know what people in these villages are!'

'Maybe,' Miss Buchanan said, opening another letter.

'He looks so refined,' Miss Stubbings mused. 'Different from the others.'

She flicked through the pages of the typescript her agent had sent. 'Of course, the gipsy may be jealous,' she said. 'He may be annoyed because we didn't show any interest in him. I think we made a mistake there, Bucky. We should have tried to make him instead of the P.B.'

She flicked through a few more pages, then she sighed:

The Jolly Garçon

'I dunno. The whole thing's completely beyond me. I feel that we'd have to stay here at least six years before we got to know him.'

'Yes, and it would take another six years to get him into bed,' Miss Buchanan said.

Miss Stubbings giggled. 'I can't wait all that long, Bucky. Life's too short!'

'Yes, and what'll he be like in another twelve years' time!' Miss Buchanan rose and gathered her letters together. 'He'll probably marry that awful cousin, have masses of ugly children and get *terribly* fat before he's thirty.'

*   *   *   *

When Miss Buchanan came back from Aylesbury, Miss Stubbings waved the typescript at her. 'It's a *wonderful* play!' she cried. 'It's much the best play I've read for years. I take poison at the end of the third act and die denouncing the *jeune fille*.'

'That's fine,' Miss Buchanan said. 'I'm glad you've come to your senses, Vi. I'll be glad to get away from Pomfret Pond. I'm a town-sparrow.

'Though I'm tired of bird-song at morning and bird-song at eve,' she said. 'That bloody cuckoo woke me at four o'clock this morning.'

'You've got no feeling for the country at all, Bucky,' Miss Stubbings reproved. 'You're deficient somewhere.'

'I don't mind,' Miss Buchanan said. 'The country isn't all it's cracked up to be.'

'I'll write to Mrs. Clifford at once and tell her to get the flat ready,' she said.

'You'll do nothing of the kind,' Miss Stubbings said. 'I've told you a thousand times I've given up the stage. I'll send this back to Gerry at once.'

'Right you are, dear,' Miss Buchanan said meekly.

The Jolly Garçon

'Will we go to the "Bugler's Call" to-night or will we go to the "Coach and Horses"?' she said at tea-time.

'I don't think we should go to either,' Miss Stubbings said. 'I'm really terribly tired of pubs. I think I'll go on the wagon.'

'I must go and see if I can get cigarettes,' Miss Buchanan said.

'I thought you got a good supply in Aylesbury?'

'Not enough to last me, ducky.'

'Well, we'll go to the "Bugler",' Violet said. 'But only for one drink.'

The brothers were playing darts when the ladies went into the pub. Chris smiled and said 'Good-evening,' but although the ladies stayed until closing-time he did not speak again. Nor did he say any more on any of the following evenings. Miss Stubbings exhausted herself (and Miss Buchanan) by speculating as to why the gipsy didn't like them.

Then one morning she said: 'I'm tired of the country. I've written to Gerry and told him I'll consider doing this play. The country really isn't all it's cracked up to be.'

'That's just what I said to Mrs Clifford,' Miss Buchanan said. 'I sent her a telegram three days ago and told her to get the flat ready.'

They smiled guiltily at each other.

'It's such a pity,' Miss Ewart said. 'He was *such* a pretty boy.'